CW00798286

AUR●RA

*Atlas Anti-Classics* 17

MICHEL LEIRIS

# AURORA

Translated and Introduced by Anna Warby

# CARDINAL POINT

Translated by Terry Hale

ATLAS PRESS LONDON

Published by Atlas Press
BCM ATLAS PRESS, LONDON WC1N 3XX

A CIP catalogue for this book is available from
The British Library
ISBN: 1 900565 46 3
ISBN-13: 978-1-900565-46-2
Printed and bound by CPI, Chippenham.
USA distribution: Artbook/DAP
www.artbook.com
UK distribution: Turnaround
www.turnaround-uk.com

# CONTENTS

## AURORA

*Introduction: The Dawning of Aurora* ... 7

Aurora ... 21

*Notes* ... 143

## CARDINAL POINT

I. Blood and Water on Every Floor ... 147
II. From the Heart to the Absolute ... 155
III. The Signal of the Arctic ... 163
IV. The Seventh Arrival of the Night ... 173

*Notes* ... 183

# INTRODUCTION: THE DAWNING OF AURORA

Appropriately enough given its title, *Aurora* was one of Leiris's earliest compositions in a literary career which spanned seven decades. That career began in 1924, the year of Breton's first Surrealist Manifesto, and Leiris was a founder member of the movement, part of that "whole little group of friends" who became Surrealists.[1] He signed the manifestos until 1929, and it was during this period of official allegiance that *Aurora* was written. Subsequently the author was associated with many different movements and literary schools of thought, but he always tended to remain on the periphery of such groups, his distance from them manifesting itself in the remarkable specificity of his work with its intense commitment to subjectivity. Despite his relatively short-lived submission to the hegemony of Breton, however, Leiris never abandoned the fundamental principles of Surrealism, clinging resolutely to its socio-political ideals while completely revising his literary methods. In some of his last interviews the author stated that in a sense he still considered himself a Surrealist: despite his formal break with the group over half a century before, Surrealism remained the most profound and enduring literary influence on Leiris's writing.

This somewhat ambiguous relationship with Surrealism, characterised by both distance and proximity, is clearly mirrored by Leiris's rather ambivalent attitude to *Aurora*. The writer on several occasions took pains to distance himself from his most obviously "Surrealist" text, a work which he chose not to publish until after the war in 1946, almost twenty years after it was written, by which time he was working closely with the existentialist and critic of Surrealism Jean-Paul Sartre, joining him on the first editorial board of *Les Temps modernes* in 1945. To this initial reluctance to publish *Aurora* Leiris added explicit criticism of the work: his 1946 preface to the novel deliberately emphasises the temporal and experiential gap separating the later writer from his much younger and therefore possibly naïve self of 1927-8 ("I was not yet thirty when I wrote *Aurora*... Today I am over forty"), and openly refers to the text as "a hotchpotch full of apparent symbolism" and "blustering prose". Later, in a letter to Adrienne Monnier on the subject of *Aurora*,[2] Leiris wrote that he felt "remote from this book" and reproached it for its aestheticism, for being too often "in the clouds".

These harsh and typically self-critical judgements have, however, been tempered by the author's lasting attachment to *Aurora*. Any hint in the preface that the work is somehow naïve because it dates from a time (before the horrors of Nazism) when the world could still be naïve is immediately refuted by its implicit suggestion that *Aurora* was in fact ahead of its time, since in a sense it foresaw those horrors, dwelling upon the dark possibilities of mankind which were to be so tragically realised in the world. Leiris was not happy, of course, to have seen *Aurora*'s predictions come to pass — prescience can be no consolation, for with hindsight the novel only emphasises the powerlessness of art — but the fact remains that this work of 1927-8 seemed *more* relevant two decades later, hence Leiris's decision that the time was ripe for its publication in 1946.

The qualities of *Aurora* which Leiris described as valuable (and which he also set out in the preface) more than compensate for the stylistic elements which irritated him, and in the context of Leiris's corpus these qualities are indeed timeless, for they remained consistently fundamental to his work. The formal character of the novel certainly differs markedly from that of his later writing. *Aurora* was written very quickly, taking only a few months to complete including lulls, and is as close as Leiris ever came to automatic writing, whereas the style of *La Règle du jeu* (The Rule of the Game), his subsequent autobiography, is characterised by constant crossing out and correction and is therefore much slower and even more tortuous, so that each of its four volumes took the best part of ten years to compose. However, the thematic concerns and general perspective of the novel testify to the consistency of Leiris, whose work in its various forms has never been anything other than an exploration and a critique of "that human condition against which some will never cease to rebel". If Leiris remained attached to this text, and if its debt to the early Surrealist vision has not fixed it in time and caused it to seem dated, then this is because *Aurora* already contains the germ of his subsequent work, both autobiographical and ethnographic. In fact these two strands of Leiris's work can never really be separated: *La Règle du Jeu*, his autobiographical masterpiece in which he finds that the writing of a life becomes life itself, partakes of ethnographic method, being composed with the use of a *fichier* or system of index cards first employed by Leiris as an ethnographer in the field. The four volumes are permeated by ethnographic themes and afford the reader particular insight into Leiris's obsession with the sort of secret or sacred language he studied in Africa (*Biffures*) and his fieldwork in the West Indies (*Fourbis*), as well as giving remarkable accounts of his trips to Communist China in 1955 (*Fibrilles*) and Cuba in 1968 (*Frêle Bruit*).

*Aurora* also partakes of the poetic method of Leiris's contemporary Surrealist work *Glossaire j'y serre mes gloses*, begun in 1925 and dedicated to his fellow dissident Surrealist Robert Desnos when published as a book in 1939.[3] This intensely subjective glossary of words juxtaposes conventional alphabetical order with the disorder of poetic significations derived from a dissection of language: Leiris literally undoes each term and reassembles its phonetic components in a different order, thereby effecting an explosion of meaning which results in highly innovative redefinitions seemingly already latent within each word. The purpose of the glossary is to challenge the oppressive, dictatorial authority of the dictionary, and its political strategy is akin to that of the critical "Dictionnaire" chronicled in *Documents* between 1929 and 1931, on which Leiris collaborated with, among others, Georges Bataille. One of Leiris's earliest and most significant contributions to this "Dictionary" was entitled "Metaphor". This entry suggests that all meaning is to some extent figurative, for it is constructed from the juxtaposition of two dissimilar entities, "language" and "thing". Language can never describe an object exhaustively; it can never claim to be entirely *objective*, but is forced to remain *partial* — both incomplete and subjective. The narrator of *Aurora* will repeat this idea in Chapter I when he states: "my language, like all language, is figurative, and… for the word 'whisky' you are quite at liberty to substitute any other term: absolute, murder, love, catastrophe or mandrake." *Glossaire* and *Aurora* both seek to demonstrate that, if all linguistic representation is more or less figurative and subjective, then the more figurative and subjective the language, the more meaningful and successful the representation. Thus the often bizarre and contradictory definitions advanced in *Glossaire* find their counterpart in the outrageous, oxymoronic metaphors of *Aurora*, where Leiris frequently forces together two utterly opposing terms. His writing is a deliberate attempt to subvert the literal signification imposed by dictionaries which, according to Leiris, arise out of a mistaken belief that words may be assigned exact meaning, a "monstrous aberration" causing men to believe that literal language facilitates human relations. This word-play, and linguistic exploration in general, has proved to be the most important mainspring of Leiris's writing.[4] *Aurora* thus marks the author's departure on a life-long journey through language, a voyage towards both self and other.

Although strictly speaking *Aurora* may not be said to adhere to the genre of autobiography, it is without doubt an intensely autobiographical novel. It stands conspicuously alone as the only work by Leiris ever to be listed under the rubric "novel". Describing the conception of *Aurora* years later in *Fibrilles* (the third volume of *La Règle du jeu*, published in 1966), the writer defines it as a "poetic novel" but one in which, he says, "I was trying to give form to my torment.'" Elsewhere Leiris suggested that he had never written a novel, lamenting his inability to create entirely fictional characters and thereby to prove that he was finally free of his obsession with the first person singular, his continual need for self-portrayal and confession. He would, he says, love to write a great novel. "But I know that I never will," he concludes. *Aurora* is certainly as close as Leiris ever came to writing fiction, but the fact remains that in this early text the author was already working towards the autobiographical mode which he would never subsequently relinquish. Thus the novel reveals Leiris experimenting with a multiplicity of voices with which to express the self, seeking the definitive autobiographical "I" with which he will become synonymous. It is significant, in view of what I shall say about the "double voyage" of *Aurora*, that this autobiographical voice was used for the first time in Africa, when Leiris kept a field diary of his initiatory ethnographic voyage (the Dakar-Djibouti Mission 1931-33). Travelling in search of the anthropological other, Leiris found himself in surprisingly close proximity to the autobiographical self.

By the time *Aurora* was published in 1946, Leiris had established himself as both a writer of autobiography and a professional ethnographer. His travel journal *L'Afrique fantôme* (Phantom Africa) appeared in 1934 and his first work of autobiography *L'Age d'homme* (Manhood) in 1939 (a new edition of this, with a prefatory essay ironically entitled "De la littérature considerée comme une tauromachie" (On Literature Considered as a Bullfight) was published in 1946, the same year as *Aurora*). In the late Thirties Leiris co-founded the Collège de Sociologie with Georges Bataille and Roger Caillois, contributing an essay on "The Sacred in Everyday Life" in which he described what the sacred meant to him personally: some of the material from this essay would reappear in the first volume of *La Règle du jeu*, *Biffures* (1948), the work which established Leiris's autobiography primarily as a representation of the subject's journey through language. In 1938 Leiris published *Miroir de la Tauromachie* (Mirror of Tauromachy) and also gained his ethnographic diploma with a dissertation on the secret or sacred language of the Dogon. The tardy publication of *Aurora* merely serves to confirm that this Surrealist novel foreshadows Leiris's nascent literary and ethnographic projects with its emphasis on the primacy of language and its thematic preoccupation with myth, ritual and sacrifice.

*Aurora* is essentially a poetic transfiguration of the journey Leiris took to Egypt and Greece from April to September 1927. Ostensibly undertaken in order to join his friend Georges Limbour who was teaching French in Cairo, this voyage was in fact motivated by a desperate need to flee Paris. Married for just over a year and working as a representative for a bookshop, Leiris began to find his bourgeois existence unbearably stifling and felt that he had utterly betrayed his Surrealist commitment, his pledge to live as a poet, to seek the absolute and to "change life" (Rimbaud). Along with many of his friends he had joined the Communist Party, but what he saw as a mere semblance of militant activity made him uneasy, and his sense of guilt was only enhanced by the aversion he felt when asked to employ his skills as a writer on the bulletin of the C.G.T., the workers' union to which he belonged. He also felt incapable of siding with either the Trotskyists or the Stalinists, swayed by the arguments of both groups, and this left him confused and more than ever conscious of his deficiencies as a revolutionary. This confusion only added to his growing personal despair which led to thoughts of suicide and worsening alcoholism. Encouraged by his wife he therefore set sail alone on the steamer *Lamartine* bound for Alexandria, in an attempt to escape the problems he hoped he was leaving behind him in Paris and follow in the footsteps of Limbour, a poet whose literary gifts and nonconformist life were an inspiration to him. This pattern would be repeated four years later when, this time on the advice of his psychoanalyst, Leiris would accept the job of "secretary-archivist" on an ethnographic mission and embark for Dakar, motivated once again by an urgent need to escape and an even more intense desire to break with his own society.

It was during his stay in Egypt that Leiris began writing *Aurora* in order to express the anguish which was evidently still very much with him. In fact the trip resulted in greater solitude than Leiris had counted on, for Limbour left Egypt to spend his summer vacation in Europe and Leiris went on alone to Greece. Far from escaping the problematic self by travelling abroad, Leiris found his isolation emphasised by his exotic surroundings. Having little money and being in any case ill-disposed to tourism, which he considered incompatible with Surrealism (this contempt for the tourist would only intensify when Leiris became an ethnographer), he led a sedentary life in Egypt with nothing to distract him from his personal preoccupations. In Chapter I of *Aurora* the narrator embarks on a long sea-crossing to an unspecified tropical land (though its distinctive features — pyramids and sand — do not leave much doubt as to the country which inspired it). By the second chapter the narrator is declaring: "We do not come into the world with impunity, and there is no possible escape." Boredom plagues the wandering couple in the text despite their marvellous voyage on horseback across the world. Their story is also a prediction of Leiris's experience in Africa where, again in spite of his location, he would find his existence sedentary, bureaucratic and dull. His field diary will confirm a truth already illustrated in *Aurora*: that the notion of travel as a means of evasion is a myth.

In Greece in 1927, however, surrounded by the veritable stuff of mythology, Leiris was busy living what he called his own "myth of the traveller". Abandoning his earlier resolve he went on an extensive tour of the country, inspecting its ancient ruins and exploring its less well-trodden parts with such zeal that the locals thought he was hunting treasure. In *Aurora* the young man in fawn leather boots searches the temple ruins in minute detail precisely in the hope of discovering hidden treasure (Chapter III). It is clear that in the following chapter the description of the vagabond also owes much to a self-portrait of Leiris roaming about Greece with only a minimum of belongings, wearing threadbare clothes, eating very frugally and finally running out of money altogether (see *Fibrilles*, p.72). The errant journey of the vagabond is also mirrored, indeed reconstructed, by the vagrant style of Leiris's text (for Montaigne, indeed, all writing was "vagabondage"): the author roams through language as he had roamed through Greece, constructing his own myths as he wanders from word to monumental word. The style of the novel moves swiftly from calm plateaux of prosaic rationality to feverish peaks of poetic delirium: in fact, the text progresses like the course of the malaria Leiris contracted towards the end of his stay in Greece, almost certainly as a direct result of his tramp-like existence. He began to feel the full effects of the disease on his return journey via Italy to France. Back in Paris he was confined to bed and in moments of extreme lucidity between hallucinations he read the *Fantômas* collection, the legendary novels celebrating the elusive anti-hero of crime who can assume an infinite variety of forms. On his recovery Leiris continued to write *Aurora*, completing it in 1928.

The narrator, the man in the white dinner-jacket, the first traveller, the vagabond, Damocles Siriel... so many avatars of the writer's errant self in search of a voice. In Chapter I the narrator relates his voyage in the first person singular, and this subjectivity only intensifies as he arrives at his destination, just as Leiris found that the self can indeed bulk large in places where one might have imagined that thoughts of the other would prevail. Despite Danton's famous exclamation to the contrary (given as his reason for not leaving France in 1794 to save himself from the guillotine), Leiris finds to his utter consternation that one does in fact "carry one's fatherland on the soles of one's shoes" (see Chapter III). As soon as the narrator writes "we had arrived," he launches into a lengthy affirmation of the subjective, confessing: "I have always found it more difficult than most to express myself other than by using the pronoun 'I'", a statement echoed by Leiris's own insistence later that he finds novel-writing impossible. Despite his impassioned argument for subjectivity ("for me this word 'I' epitomises the structure of the world"), a desperate struggle to avoid submitting to the fearful "third person" equated with death which negates the existence of every individual and renders it absurd, the narrator none the less imposes upon himself the law of objectivity at the end of Chapter I, assuming the traditional role of the omniscient storyteller, an invisible but all-seeing observer ("Here, however, on this island where I have just come ashore, the first person singular is no longer of prime importance and I must grant a voice to the dynamite of events"). Arriving in the Tropics, the narrator is a forerunner of Leiris the secretary-archivist who was to arrive in Africa, mindful of ethnographic protocol and his professional duty to report only the facts and to leave aside the self in order to observe the other. In practice, however, Leiris would find the science's dismissal of subjectivity unacceptable, indeed absurd, and his field diary *L'Afrique fantôme* would act as textual dynamite in the explosion of this myth of objectivity. The publication of this intimate journal signified a clear breach of discipline within the Marcel Griaule 'school' to which Leiris supposedly belonged: it provoked a major scandal and put an end to the friendship between the two men. Leiris's preoccupation with the subjective experience of the ethnographer was completely at odds with Griaule's teamwork ethic, which regarded the individual researcher as an intelligent cog in a collective — and objective — ethnographic machine. For Leiris, on the other hand, the ethnographer is himself his only tool of observation, and since he is inevitably implicated in the ethnographic encounter it is essential that he accept his subjectivity and indeed scrutinise the ethnographic self. Leiris suggests that maximum subjectivity is in fact the only means of access to objectivity: his ethnography thus adheres to — and is a continuation of — the same principle governing the early poetry of *Glossaire*, namely that intense subjectivity facilitates and advances human communication rather than precluding it. Certain of Leiris's colleagues at the Musée de l'Homme never forgave him his unorthodox insistence on painting a rigorously honest picture of the "ethnographic self" of the Mission (including, of course, its more dubious practices): it is unlikely that the Vichy government of 1940 would have been aware of *L'Afrique fantôme* had one of those colleagues not alerted the authorities to its existence. They then destroyed all remaining copies of its first edition, regarding Leiris's strong anti-colonialist conviction as subversive. Today, notions of ethnographic reflexivity are fashionable, and Leiris's work has undoubtedly played a large part in this gradual acceptance of subjectivity within the discipline. Seventy years ago, however, the author of *L'Afrique fantôme* was considered a heretic.

The attempt to write "objectively", or more precisely to write of the self as a third person, is all but abandoned in the third chapter of *Aurora* in favour of the explicitly autobiographical "I" of Damocles Siriel. By dint of the anagram Siriel, Leiris is clearly identified with this unsavoury, Sadean anti-hero. In fact the play on his name dates from a childhood game when Leiris and his brothers would pretend to be fairground entertainers, the eldest of the three, Jacques, announcing the attractions to the public and presenting the young Pierre and Michel as, respectively, Siriel Piar the Hungarian violin virtuoso and Julian Lechim the lion-tamer. In memory of these prestigious performers Leiris reverses his surname to construct the murderous hierarch Siriel, replacing the name Lechim by that of Damocles after the mythical courtier who in the midst of a lavish feast beheld above his head a heavy sword suspended by a single hair and was thus made to understand the precarious nature of happiness and the vulnerability of the mighty. It is therefore fitting that the character of this name in the novel should come to grief just when he is certain that his position of absolute power is unassailable. By using the name Damocles, Leiris can simultaneously elevate himself to mythical status and express his inner torment and sense of impending doom. The single thread from which the sword dangles menacingly is of course symbolically present in the novel in the form of a wisp of blond hair. Siriel is literally Leiris's mirror-image, an autobiographical writer who resolves to tell his story in its most intimate and self-condemnatory details. He prefigures the confessional content of *L'Age d'homme*, an explicit and often humiliating self-representation which Leiris published in the hope of posing some sort of literary threat to himself, in an attempt to risk bringing the blade of Damocles ever nearer, to construct a textual "shadow of the bull's horn" or, seen from the point of view of the bull as victim (to which Leiris also likens himself), a shadow of the sword with which the matador will deliver the final *estocada*.

Further confirmation that *Aurora* represents the crystallisation of Leiris's autobiographical project is provided by the author's pencil drawing of 1928 entitled *Ma vie par moi-même* (My life, by myself). The sketch depicts three things: a pyramid standing in front of the horizon, Leiris's profile turned towards this object and a woman's eye gazing at Leiris from beneath long, wavy hair. The image evidently owes a great deal to the novel with which it is contemporary. Indeed a textual version of the drawing appears at the end of Chapter II in the tripartite description of Aurora, her flame-like locks flowing as she momentarily turns to look at her companion, the geometric figure of the pyramid and the white man who seems to be of stone and who is eventually left standing alone in the desert. The drawing was intended to symbolise Leiris's sense of radical isolation. There is a small but unbridgeable gap between the male figure and the cold, inaccessible shape of the pyramid at which he stares; equally, there can be no contact between the man and the woman despite the latter's gaze, which would suggest that she seeks an impossible union with him. Leiris would go on to call this the condition of the poet, destined to remain "eternally separate". Since in his opinion the true ethnographer is also a poet, it comes as no surprise to find that this is also an image of ethnographic isolation. *Aurora* might indeed be said to evoke the condition of *dépaysement* (literally, disorientation specifically provoked by a change of country) and *Ma vie par moi-même* certainly foreshadows another triangular configuration, to be found in *L'Afrique fantôme*, which describes the experience of insurmountable distance between self and other, between one world and another. Here the ethnographer Leiris is completely excluded from the triangle, trapped within the closed circle of the self ("I look at these three things: Abba Jérôme's notebook, the sheep's diaphragm and Emawayish's bare knee, and more than ever I am aware of my irremediable isolation. It's as if these three points, forming a triangle in my head... cut the world around me with a knife as if to separate me from it and imprison me forever in the circle (incomprehensible or absurd for anyone else) of my own enchantments," *L'Afrique fantôme*, p.407).

What, then, of this "other" in the text, of Aurora herself? The eponymous heroine of the novel would seem to be the object of both poetic and ethnographic desire. At the inception of the work the narrator hears the whispered word "Aurora" and this sound, not yet revealed as a proper name, is the catalyst of his departure on a long journey, the voyage through space and language which produces the text of *Aurora*. In the beginning is the generative poetic word "Aurora", a mysterious feminine utterance which carries the subject off as if by magic into the distant unknown. In the second chapter Aurora is revealed to be the name of a woman, and this woman is the embodiment of the poetic force which initiated the subject's departure, for it is her identity which the traveller seeks to know. She would also seem to be a personification of the sacred as Leiris defines it, for she is clearly a "coincidence of contradictions," and the hyperbolical, humorously bizarre description of her has the effect of posing the problem of her identity rather than resolving it ("This woman was that lighter... This woman was that coincidence... This woman was at the same time that absence and that link... This woman was that point and its transposition", etc.).[5] She is, in fact, an enigma, eternally ambiguous and indefinable. In his letter to Monnier, Leiris writes that Aurora is a figure representing that which is beyond our grasp, an image of all that we yearn for in vain. For this reason he cites as an epigraph to the novel a distich from "Les Cydalises", one of Nerval's *Odelettes* (1852) — an expression of his love for impossible loves ("Where are our sweethearts? /They are in the grave"). The forename Aurora designates for Leiris "an eminently universal, timeless creature whose only distinct characteristic is that she is a stranger who comes from 'another world' (in the social as well as in the mystical sense of the phrase)." She is a product of the author's desire to escape from the self into an entirely different culture, the desire which would lead him to become an ethnographer. Like the ethnographic object, she promises to provide "the future scene of a fresh embrace," the dawning of a new day (Aurora: goddess of the dawn).

In her *Souvenirs de Londres*, Monnier had wondered whether Leiris's novel might have been inspired by the work of the Pre-Raphaelite painter Edward Burne-Jones, whose *Aurora* (1896) shows a woman with cymbals walking barefoot beside a canal just before daybreak. In fact, however, Leiris first saw this painting a long time after writing the novel. His inspiration was purely literary, for Aurora is also a Nervalian collage, her name deriving from the fusion of Aurelia and Pandora. Both these names appear in *Glossaire j'y serre mes gloses*, confirming that the novel is an extension of this word-play:

> AURELIA — *Or il y a* [Gold there is] (*Glossaire*, p.75)
> PANDORA — *qui se pendra l'aura!* [whoever hangs himself will have her!] (*Glossaire*, p.103)

From the start Aurora is therefore a literary double, and by the close of the work she has become a multiplicity of feminine essences (Dora, Diana, Anna, Flora) with all of whom the traveller is in love but none of whom he may possess. For Aurora resists possession and definition, and the text bears witness to the impossibility of fixing her in language, of naming her and understanding her meaning. She is like the elusive Philosophers' Stone whose avatars are innumerable, and her name gives rise to many glosses (Eau-Rô-Râh, OR AURA, OR AUX RATS, O'RORA), emphasising this lack of fixity. The horror of fixity manifested by *Aurora* is, we recall from the preface, one of the qualities of the novel most valued by Leiris. A personification of the poetic *Glossaire* (whose deliberate juxtaposition of clashing terms, which literally make contradictions coincide, is therefore revealed as part of the author's attempt to reinstate the sacred in Western language), she transgresses logic and grammar, replacing them with her own secret language or "hieroglyphics".

The quest for Aurora is destined to fail: for Leiris the only true meeting-point of self and other is death. At times in this apocalyptic tale we are not far from Conrad's

*Heart of Darkness*: the narrator's desperate plea to the heroine in Chapter V ("Aurora! Aurora!") is reminiscent of Kurtz's dying exclamation, "The horror! The horror!", and indeed by the end of the text "Aurora" will have been transformed into "HORRORA", precisely as the vagabond dies. The end of the novel marks the end of a journey, and the narrator's homecoming is less than triumphant. His humble return to Paris confirms that nothing has changed, that still greater enigmas remain to be solved "at the source", i.e. within the traveller himself. The problematic self literally resurfaces (in the Seine), and the writer embarks on another journey closer to home, which results in the highly introspective 'staircase episode'. Although this text serves as a prologue to the novel, it was in fact written slightly later than *Aurora* and was originally intended to be the start of another novel which was subsequently abandoned. This nightmarish narrative — inspired by the real staircase he used every day while living in Boulogne-sur-Seine — is an elaborate metaphor for the author's descent into the hellish self, his reflexive journey down through his humiliating body towards his own dark heart.

Towards the other, towards the self: voyages which, for Leiris, were ultimately indistinguishable. The quest for knowledge of the other is necessarily a process of exchange in which the questioning self is entirely implicated: in the work of Leiris autobiography and ethnography are part of a single anthropological project. He continued to pursue the other, and his self-representation remained a crucial dimension of that pursuit. As another writer puts it, "the most singular part of the self is always the most universal part."[6] In *Aurora* we catch a glimpse of the writer at the very outset of a double journey which was to prove the motive force of his exceptional career.

## NOTES

1. Leiris describes his early literary influences in an interview with Madeleine Gobeil in *Sub-Stance* 11-12 (1975), p.45ff. In the same issue there is a useful article by Renée Riese Hubert entitled "Aurora: Adventure in word and image", pp.74-87.
2. See Adrienne Monnier, *Souvenirs de Londres: Petite suite anglaise avec une lettre de Michel Leiris*, Mercure de France, 1957, pp.99-106.
3. The glossary previously appeared in three issues of *La Révolution surréaliste*: no. 3 (April 1925, with a preface by Leiris and a note by Artaud), no. 4 (July 1925) and no. 6 (March 1926). The 1939 *Glossaire j'y serre mes gloses* can be found in *Mots sans mémoire*, Gallimard, 1969, pp.71-116.
4. The continuing importance of *Glossaire* was emphasised by the publication of *Langage Tangage* (1985) which includes a supplement to it. In the same year the inclusion of another version of *Glossaire* in the major ethnological review *Études rurales* was an indication that Leiris's literary works, considered aberrant and marginal in the 1930s, were finally beginning to be reinstated within the discipline to which they also belong. *Glossaire*'s poetic revolution has thus helped revolutionise the ethnographic text. See Michel Leiris, "Glanes", *Études rurales* 97-98 (1985), pp.25-32.
5. For Leiris the sacred is characterised by its fundamental ambiguity. It is, as he writes in "The Sacred in Everyday Life", "something simultaneously attractive and dangerous, prestigious and outcast", and it inspires at once "respect, desire and terror". See Denis Hollier [ed.], *The College of Sociology (1937-39)*, University of Minnesota Press, 1988, p.24.
6. Marguerite Duras, in an interview in *Le Nouvel Observateur* (28 September 1984, p.53).

# AURORA

## AUTHOR'S PREFACE

And I was hoping for the end of the world
But for me the end approaches whistling like a hurricane.
GUILLAUME APOLLINAIRE

I was not yet thirty when I wrote *Aurora* and the world had not yet known the Nazi plague. It was not really in bad faith that I called for an apocalypse and held mankind up to public derision. Today I am over forty and mankind has known apocalypse and damnation. I have been no more delighted by this than anyone else.

Even though *Aurora* is a hotchpotch full of apparent symbolism, and despite the "black" or "frenetic" style of its blustering prose, what I like about this work is the appetite it expresses for an unattainable purity, the faith it places in the untamed imagination, the horror it manifests with regard to any kind of fixity — in fact, the way almost every page of it refuses to accept that human condition against which some will never cease to rebel, however reasonably society may one day be ordered.

It was midnight when the idea occurred to me of going down into that gloomy antechamber hung with old etchings and suits of armour. The worn furniture lay slumbering in corners and the carpets were quietly mouldering, gradually eroded by an acid different from the *aqua fortis* which had eaten into the matrices from which the etchings had first emerged. This acid was dispersed in the air like the acrid and melancholy smell of animal suint, reminiscent of faded old linen.

Time was passing over my head with the chilling treachery of a draught. My ears were still buzzing with the sound of solemn words, and saliva from my gums moistened my teeth which felt as though they had come loose, so lifeless were my jaws. I expected nothing and hoped for still less. At most, all I felt was that by moving to a different room on another floor I would bring about an imaginary rearrangement of the organs in my body and thus of the thoughts in my mind.

I felt neither emotion nor pain; nothing concerned me except perhaps the fear of colliding with the furniture. I literally dragged myself along, with my eyes — or rather my hair — about five foot six inches above the carpet. My penis felt diluted, as if reduced to water or to the powder of decaying bones. I stood upright, my legs like two monoliths swaying in the middle of a desert and my arms swinging loosely like the strings of a whip, hanging corpses, or two windmills. My chest rose and fell as I breathed and I could feel the heaviness of my innards weighing me down as mournfully as a suitcase filled, not with clothing, but with butcher's meat.

Was this, then, where so much pride was ultimately to lead? Was this the metal buffer into which everything which might have made me remotely human would run, like a train at high speed? I continued my descent towards that sinister antechamber, moving slowly down a staircase with no bannister, but edged instead with a cord the colour of old rose which filled me with a rising nausea I found impossible to suppress. A few more steps and I would no longer be treading on carpet, having reached the stone floor.

The flagstones were rigidly balanced, linked to each other as are the pans of a pair of scales: small dishes made of copper, silver or an alloy of some kind and loaded with bags of sand strictly equal in weight, so that there would be not the slightest point in pitting them against each other for, given this perfect match, the contest would inevitably end in a draw. The floor showed no trace of this invisible battle — real none the less — and I was only made aware of it by the beating of my heart which now and then made a vague clanking sound whenever a strange breeze rattled the panoplies. On the right-hand wall hung an ancient, rusty breastplate lightly inlaid with a representation of some story, a rebus left colourless by the demise of the symbol which had disappeared noiselessly underground one evening, the guests of that night having paid not the slightest heed to its fate. Against the left-hand wall there stood an annoying sideboard too plainly wrought to be in the least bit engaging to the eye. This sideboard was blind, deaf and dumb, its wood roughened and pierced with holes, a veritable termites' nest bored into an earth of silence, that most unfeeling of materials lacking both consistency and substance.

A few inches above my head time was passing, slipping by parallel to the flagstones and flowing along the walls of the corridors, slavishly following their contours even into the most unlikely nooks and crannies. Now and then a tiny mouse fled in fear, even though I trod warily, with hesitant, muffled footsteps which perfectly mirrored the furniture around me, lost in its motionless dream from which it could only be awakened by some fantastic clock with a face of white clouds and hands of concentrated lightning.

For twenty years I had not dared venture down this maze of a staircase, for twenty years I had been shut away, imprisoned within the peeling walls of the old attic. A hundred times the spiders had spun their webs and a hundred times I had torn them down, only for them to begin again. The room in which I remained made me pointlessly dizzy, and all day long I leant against the wall to prevent myself from falling.

"So it is I who am this pathetic recluse," I thought, "and though my hands may be no more than two birds of prey, even so their talons are not sharp enough to act as anything other than the bars of a railing to which I can cling like a common drunkard. Though the four winds may roar in the immediate vicinity of my meninges and the ends of my hair, and though the lightning which rises on certain days from decomposing corpses may illuminate my face with its great phosphorescent flashes, still I persist in rotting in this horrible attic. What a confusion of worm-eaten floorboards, ransacked cupboards, cheap pitch-pine tables, dirty dishes, filthy birds and dusty albums, casting a constant stream of spells upon me and from which no jolt could ever set me free! The doors turn on their hinges and the hangings stir, but I hardly notice as I sink ever deeper into the floor's merciless swamp. The wooden boards turn to mud and there my feet take root, my legs wither and soon nothing will remain of my body, since it bears no mark of greatness or immortality. My knees knock together, my teeth chatter with fear and my eyes are like flies hurling themselves into every spider's web. Insatiable insects, will you have done with torturing me! I wish I were a strong and scarlet-faced hunter with toes heavy in boots. The sound of my gunfire would make the thunder yellow with envy, the rain would turn to urine and all autumn long the sky would keep on pissing like a terrified animal innocently emptying its bladder with no concern for your stupid etiquette fit only for what men really are — animals who refrain from excreting."

One fine evening, however, I decided to leave this attic. Shaking as I lit a lamp, I ventured out on to the dark mineshaft of the staircase. I watched the projection of my shadow along the walls; it looked like the traces of antediluvian plants such as those found etched like metal ore into rock fissures, dark manchineel trees whose sap is a dangerous fire-damp set to explode horribly any moment a spark should come near its poison.

Step by step I slowly descended the stairs. An occasional crack, like the sound of a match being struck, conjured thousands of memories within me. I was very old and each event I recalled ran up through the innermost core of my muscles like errant screw-taps inside a piece of furniture or lichen climbing to attack a statue. I was not leaning on a stick but was supported by the lamp I carried in my right hand, its tall flame reaching as high as possible to lick the ceiling, urging me with its caresses and by some secret bond to follow its upward movement.

The stairs groaned under my feet, and I felt as though I were wading through the deep-red blood of wounded animals whose guts were the weft of the soft carpet. It was the result of a very cruel hunt — an entire herd of deer had been run down. The horns sounded as the hounds barked and devoured their prey. The twitching carcasses diminished with every passing second, torn to pieces by so many fangs. Only the skeletons remained and the strangely sculptured antlers whose irregular structures stretched up into the darkness with the same number of branches as their years, skyscrapers rising storey by storey and share issue by share issue until they literally scraped the clouds, so as to spread among all things the scab consuming their bases — a scab undoubtedly less gentle than the orient of a pearl necklace which one also adds to pearl by pearl and year after year.

The forests moaned as the packs of hounds ran through them in a frenzy. Leaves were whipped from the trees. Bushes were forced apart like the thighs of someone being raped. All the ponds were emptied, sucked dry by so many voracious mouths, and all the animals whirled round and round in a terrifying carousel in the dim light of the stars looking anxiously down to see what horn played upon a chasm or a comet would one day sound their death-note. A woman dressed in red tucked hocks cut from the roebucks into the tops of her polished boots, thus transforming her legs, which were tightly wrapped in white skin, into wonderful vases of flowers fragrant with the delicate scent of blood. A castle of grey stone and glowing red brick loomed up on the horizon. The entire hunt surged in through its gigantic double gates which clanged shut with a single gong-like sound — a death-knell for the animals they had killed. All that remained in the forest were a few bones, echoes of the hounds' barking and a very long trail of drops of blood shed one by one by the fleeing herd of deer, red pebbles less difficult to see than Hansel's white stones...[1]

But no — I really cannot stay upright on such a staircase any longer! In the end I am too afraid, and the flame in my lamp is not a strong enough support. What I need are several breastplates, a criss-cross of swords and a jungle of armchairs behind which to hide. If now there is no other way I can possibly go down the stairs except on all fours, then it is because coursing through my veins is the same ancestral red river which once gave life to the throbbing mass of all these hunted beasts. A position outwardly resembling that of a quadruped is the one which most befits me, for it is certainly preferable, as far as safety is concerned, to have four feet instead of two — indeed, even to be a centipede, a worm or a spider.

I was on all fours then, with my hands a few inches lower than my feet because I had not yet quite completed my descent, and ahead of me more steps presented themselves covered in a cheap woollen fabric with brass stair-rods marking out their hollow right-angles with hard, rigid lightning flashes that were not even allowed to zigzag. Strange murmurings continued to rise within me, and I listened to the huge sorrows that swelled the houses with their forge-sized bellows, blowing open the doors and windows to make craters of sadness which, coloured a dirty yellow by the sickly glow of the family lamps, belched forth an inexhaustible stream of soup mixed with sounds of quarrelling, bottles being uncorked by sweating hands and chewing. A long river of fillet steaks and badly cooked vegetables flowed out. Broths the colour of sour wine saw the despair of children swimming away amidst their greasy waters heavy with eyes of fat which were only half awake. The window panes steamed up with a veil of mist which the brows of adolescents did not wipe away when they pressed against them as soon as the tables were cleared. They turned their backs on their mothers who, though doubtless active were forever paralysed, caught up in eternal mending and sweeping. Bloodthirsty towns! What fortifications built by a mercenary in league with the grasping fingers of some demented lawyer clasp you tightly in their odious girdle!

All the birds will die of hunger, or else, spreading their irritated wings, will fly away to healthier parts, if such may be found outside this continent which resembles a ghastly pillory in which life is forever trapped...

I continued to go down stair by stair, and I had now come to the last two steps. They stretched before me, cold and exact, fixed in glacial, ironic immobility. The sea of black and white flagstones died away at the foot of their cliff very close by, and I dreaded the moment when, with only my hands and knees for a raft, I would have to leap on to this element which, though flat and hard, was secretly disturbed by violent eddies.

To the left of the antechamber stood a half-open door through which a lumber-room could be seen, full of entire generations of assorted objects, like one of those ship-chandler's stores which abound in ports. Old corsets, mixed with piles of what were once dance cards, dried flowers and threadbare silk dresses, lay side by side with moth-eaten scraps of fur, fans gnawed away till they resembled ducks' feet stripped of their webbing, wonderfully exquisite and delicate silver shoes which had lost both soles and heels, the remains of a feast and two or three little stuffed dogs tangled up in packets of fish-hooks and balls of string. Heaps of shadow covered all these things. The objects protruded like mountain-tops emerging from the clouds when a sudden gust of wind tears open the screen that was hiding them from view. The shapes revealed their peaks and troughs like mountain-sides, and pulsated like animal bodies swathed in dark skin. This muddle of contours and irregular-shaped humps and ridges was no different from a stormy night and even exuded a sort of aroma like a sunken lane or a wet road.

Among the objects piercing the darkness could be seen an old wax statue of the Virgin Mary, next to a crystal ball like the one which marked the beginning of the stair-rail, and close to one of those colossus lamp-stands in the shape of a group of negroes with shining black skin, loin-cloths around their hips, their mouths glowing with barbaric laughter and a chain about their necks.

Tropical storms always come down on crops of buckwheat or maize without warning. With all possible speed the workers desert the fields. They gather up their meagre tools and keeping their eyes fixed on their huts they run for shelter. More than one of them will squeeze tightly in his hand an incomprehensible ju-ju as he utters ancestral prayers, while at the same time taking care to avoid the hedges, ditches and obstacles of every kind which lie in his path. His wife is a magnificent creature whose bare chest glistens all the more after the shower's caress, and whose high breasts are made still more erect by the soft touch of the warm rain which is more delicious than the touch of callous hands accustomed to manipulating primitive tools. This beautiful black giantess striding majestically with her strong, sturdy legs presents her amorous bosom to the thunder, the two points standing out, extended to their full length and taut to the point of extraordinary metallic hardness, two lightning-conductor tips eager only to attract the lightning, as if nothing but the sudden electric embrace of clouds charged with catastrophe could assuage their desire after so many long, wet, delicate kisses.

In the huts they go straight to bed, stop up their ears or else fall to their knees before some little statue of a virgin or saint brought there by a missionary. If necessary they sacrifice a sheep, and the youngest of the nubile girls immerses herself completely in a bath of blood from which she emerges coloured crimson and half-intoxicated. In Africa the tom-toms beat; in America harmoniums sing and between Harlem and Guinea strange currents are set up. Last night the whites, who were drunk, massacred three women from one village who refused to sleep with them because they feared this very storm, and because nothing on Earth would have made them submit to the embrace of a male before taking their bath of blood. In the end the colonial brutes forced it on them all the same, but they were dead and scarcely concerned by such attentions. At the same moment, at the very top of a skyscraper, a fair mulatto woman was diving naked into a bath filled to the brim with a mixture of gin and whisky. She too emerged completely drunk and began singing in a perfectly frenetic voice, with a gravelly tone that gave goose-pimples to the pebbles on even the most distant pathways, arm movements that turned the Poles and the Equator upside down, lips as fresh as milk and foot-tapping wild enough to set the thunder rolling... Then, when all the men present had more or less taken advantage of her, this woman quietened down.

She put her dress back on, arranged her hair and left, clutching to her bosom a scapular, the only precious gift her mother had given her before sending her out into the wide world with half a dollar and her blessing. The songs this mouth had uttered would remain eternally etched on the air and have their effect on all phenomena, from the rise in the price of cotton to the flowering of chrysanthemums in greenhouses, and even the temperature of the lumber-room where the oddments I am talking about reigned supreme: dance shoes, corsets, balls of string and a giant standard lamp…

Ship-chandlers' stores have always held a prodigious fascination for me, even more so than secondhand shops and ironmongers' stores. Their resemblance to a junk-room gives the impression that the sea has washed up everything it did not want, clean and tidy pieces of flotsam it has not yet consumed, and greatly appeals to someone like me, who is unable to conceive of the world except as a vast enclosure in which we have piled up assorted refuse fit for making who knows what extravagant compost-heap. A sailor's blue tunic on which thick cork floats are placed, along with trouser buttons, gold braid, proud anchors and nets so fine and delicate that one could only imagine their being used in the air: these form to my eyes a splendid panorama which I find perhaps less tiresome than the spectacles of nature, for I am but an odious aesthete more accustomed to the lifeless, stinking atmosphere of store-cupboards and attics than to sea breezes. This love of objects, or rather this obsession with them shared by dilettantes and artists, is something I only ever admit to with great shame, and most of the time I content myself with trying to disguise it by means of magical justifications or stories like this one. To tell the truth, I cling to inanimate objects like a passenger clinging to the rail of a steamship on a very stormy day — a much more flattering comparison for me than that of a mussel glued to its rock.

In this case, the rail to which I clung was in fact the edge of the last step on the staircase. It was not even the stair-rail which offered me its pathetic support but the step itself, much lower down and more befitting the terrible uneasiness that gripped me. Like a mutineer clapped in irons I remained motionless, and even the approach of a red-hot cannon-ball would not have prompted me to move either backwards or forwards. Like a mutineer clapped in irons, or rather a tottering missionary seized by pirates.

It must by now have been about two o'clock in the morning, and outside all was quiet. Not a single carriage went past. The pure, icy air was undisturbed by any mewing cat or wailing siren in search of a mysterious cargo in some far-off port. It would have been nice to hear the sudden resounding crash of piles of plates, but the air was devoid of any violent cascade of china rending the atmospheric strata like a peal of laughter indicating absolute madness. I thought of my mother, my childhood and the identical silence which had been pierced by horrible screams the night I was brought into the world.

Blacker than a beast, dark and creaking like a rotten barouche, you walk or rather dawdle through the outskirts of life, with your chewed thumbs whose skin you have been devouring for countless numbers of years. Little by little you lacerate these fingers, which others use for tender caresses, violent battles or stubborn labours; you strip them bare as if wishing to leave only the bones and to redeem, by the tithe of suffering you thus inflict upon yourself, the threat of greater and more dangerous torments hovering over you like a vampire. Your friends? You dislike them. In fact, you like nobody. You are just a man going down the stairs...

This staircase is not the vertical passage with spiralling steps which allows access to the various parts of the premises housing your attic, but your innards themselves, the digestive tract which connects your mouth (of which you are proud) with your anus (of which you are ashamed), hollowing out a sticky, sinuous trench right through your body. Each particle of food you swallow slips down to the bottom of this duct and so it is you yourself — potentially, at least — who are going down the staircase with timorous, measured steps, falling slowly and in terror just as you fell from that empyreal sky, your mother's womb, a parcel of flesh bouncing from cloud to cloud between the mortal towers of two contorted legs.

Neither are these stairs — so reassuring after all in their geometrical precision — the worthy steps by which you descend to the ground from the height of your thoughts, for they continually let you down and bring you day by day closer to an icy corridor filled with old scarecrows so tragic that on seeing them the idea of suicide drops on to your shoulders and stays there, clinging more tenaciously than a leaden chasuble.

And all your life you will be going down this staircase.

The poems you will write, the stupid things you will say, everything which will or will not happen to you, the pleasures you will enjoy and the tortures you will suffer: all this will be no more real to you than any one of the different phantoms which at this very moment dwell in the darkness of the staircase, whose slope alone is bloody and real. Though you might be in the heart of Paris, London or any other capital, it is no more true than if you had never been there and it little matters what you do, say or write, since all intellectual output is merely foolish literature composed after the event by what you might call (very amusingly in this case and why on Earth, great heavens, should we not joke?) "*l'esprit de l'escalier*"...[2]

What you need is to return to swallowing large bowlfuls of air at a single gulp — a punch from a fist or a stab from a knife — without being restrained in any way by these excruciating subtleties with their absurd hair-splitting.

Without even realising it, however, having crawled on your stomach a few yards along the corridor, you have just found this bowlful of air in the shape of the door which opens on to the street and which, with one nudge of the head, without a word, and with your gums and teeth clenched, you have just burst abruptly open.

. . . . . . . . . . . . . . . . . . . . . . . . . . . . . . . . . . . . . . . . . . . . . . . . . . . . . . . . . . . . . .

# I.

*Where are our sweethearts?*
*They are in the grave.*
GÉRARD DE NERVAL

I was standing in front of a wooden plaque and I saw its sinuous lines forming rosettes like flowers of truth. Not far away a woman in modest attire was sitting on the newest bench of an old square, which was full of the stench of children dragging their hoops and their mothers behind them. This woman was rather plain but her eyes, veritable torches of wretchedness, were reflected in a cloud which had formed neither high nor low.

On the plaque I read the account of several episodes past or still to come, as if its knots and graining had been hieroglyphics simplified in the extreme. I was advancing through its ligneous waves, pushing aside with both hands the lianas and brushwood of fact, in order to see the whole history of the world reflected in its absolute reality on the frosted glass, the pure and bare inner surface, when the woman, rising with a sudden but graceful movement, having smoothed out the creases in her crumpled skirt with little touches of her slender hand, took three steps in the direction of a lawn and solemnly greeted the grape harvests of the future which were coming towards her in the form of hailstones. Then I heard the word: "Aurora," whispered in a gentle voice softer than despairing flesh, and I felt the asphalt pontoon that was carrying me and my plaque, so rich in secrets, cast off and begin to glide between two stone quays whose hard arms — scarecrows of insufficient length — became semaphore signals raised in the vain hope of holding me back.

A horizon of white stone set down like the abstract line closing the metaphysical operation of departure (subtraction of memories, addition of new pleasures, multiplication of the future, division of most recent desires) — this horizon, inscribed like a marble stela, was the boundary post of my vision and I began to hear the wash of many waves, bushes of lightning which had been reduced to a liquid mass but none the less retained, if not the fire's burning flame, then at least the fiery pride of its zigzags. The pontoon danced onwards and I felt the fixed point being tossed about in my head, the fixed point which nothing can shake loose and which mercilessly tears us apart when our actions or passions convey a movement to our brains and bodies that is at variance with the direction in which the eternal steel needle points, immutable as a nail in the wall or the centre of reference which turns any restless movement into a flow of blood through its continuous yet immovable friction. On either side of me streams fell apart, and I listened to their faint sound with a slight sneer of superiority — I who was striding above this tide, dragging with me, much to the detriment of the universe, the entire range of my perceptions, my backwash of vinegar and my leafy landmarks, to the top of the trees of knowledge at whose summit my love is engendered.

A strangely assorted crew filled the dark sides of the pontoon. Men of every colour were bustling about stoking enormous fires at such a depth that everything down there merged into a sort of blackish mist like undifferentiated matter. On deck, gigantic women's heads emerged, all facing towards the stone horizon, and it was possible to calculate the speed of the boat from the angle of their hair. These women, who seemed to me like marvellous living statues, must have been submerged in the water up to their waists (only the upper half of their bodies being inside the vessel) and it must have been their legs alone which, underwater, generated the ship's movement, the deep fires having been lit by the crew for the sole purpose of some mysterious adoration, while the watery whiteness of the flesh of these giantesses inexorably drew the marble horizon towards them, one lip of a wound attracting the other lip to erase the sea like a scar, in accordance with the principle that like attracts like.

There is no need for me to relate the various vicissitudes of this voyage, for they are all more or less recounted in the tales of ancient seafarers. All the storms, charmed into submission by the women's beauty, grew calm like weary animals and came gently to lap at their breasts. The great sea-serpents coiled themselves up again, content to mark out the ship's course like heaps of horse-dung, and even the octopuses were merely skilled insects weaving thousands of intersecting currents which our voyage was to unravel, Gordian knots which the ship untied like Alexander, transforming its prow into drapers' shears which unhesitatingly cut a single straight line through the fine silk cloth of the day.

Of all our ports of call during this crossing I remember only one, whose magical bars tore open the entrails of the town and allowed the divine haruspices of alcohol to observe, through the sides of their glasses in which the streets were reflected, the fatal outcome of carnal encounters when the sexes sharpen themselves like knives on the grindstone of the senses. The most brightly lit of these bars, in which the drinks unleashed the most piercing thunderbolts, stood at the end of a narrow alley and the rugged, uneven cobblestones marking its threshold frustrated the most devout desires, their rough curves incapable of simulating the smooth dome of a stomach. The name of this place was "The Parts of the Body Rendezvous" and indeed the regulars scrupulously observed the custom of only going there with their bodies completely covered except for one single part, which differed for each person and which could be any scrap of the human carcass: a hand, a foot, a mouth, an ear or even just a finger segment. The women were subject to this common rule, and they too veiled the whole of their bodies apart from one particular part which they deemed the most beautiful, thus adding their members to these assemblies of fragments invisibly presided over by a dissector's knife.

On a night thick with frenzied insects and the swell of splintered panes of glass, I left my room in the ship's hold with the intention of venturing into this den, and I was quick to cover my whole body using a black cloth made from the thickest fibres of my wooden plaque so that only my left elbow remained visible, as smooth as a stone. Once inside, I was offered various beverages in which I could see different bodily organs in the process of fermenting round sugar crystals which were forming into vague skeletons. A light froth overflowed the goblet, and I could easily imagine how wildly drunk it would make me, merely at the sight of its extravagant whiteness and the infinitely varied bubbles rising from it, little spherical statues of the colours, exhumed after the death of reason which was dry and had been beaten to dust like plaster. With the first glass I drank, the invisible dissector appeared, hoisting up his blood-red face like a star, and his knife whistled through the air, embedding itself in the floor right in the middle of the bar. With my second glass, both men and women discarded their veils and I saw that they were not in fact either men or women, but in reality solely the bodily parts which as seeming individuals they were supposed to represent. With my third glass, all the lights flickered and the knife, which had placed itself in the most delicate and transparent of hands, tore through the room in every direction, cutting the air as if wishing to complete the dissection, while in every glass the drinks turned red, thickened suddenly and immediately stopped frothing. With my fourth glass I realised that, since unlike my partners I was not merely a part of the body but a real human being and in every sense alive, my position was extremely dangerous and that consequently, on pain of an ignominious death, I must take flight immediately. With my fifth glass, however, I noticed that the door (tall enough when I entered to let me through without my having even to stoop) had also just divided into several parts and that now, while it was still possible for each of my limbs to make use of this exit separately, I certainly could not leave with my body intact. All hope of escape had therefore to be dismissed, banished to a remote corner of my brain along with the rotten remains of old ruses and the saltpetre of defunct stage shows. It was then that panic set in between my head and the ceiling with its wings of thick dust, and I only had eyes for the movements of the knife.

For some time I had lain in a corner prostrate with fear, expecting at any moment to be torn to pieces by the moving blade, when I felt the silken touch of hair winding itself round my elbow which was still bare, while at the same time a mysterious fragrance wafted up to my nostrils. I closed my eyes for a moment under the spell of this unexpected caress — undoubtedly the last, I believed, which I would be capable of feeling — but when I reopened them I realised that I was in the street, away from the dangers of that inhuman bar. A few steps away from me the knife was zigzagging up into the sky, lightning returning to its source, while a wisp of fair female hair flew straight up into the air, soon merging with the colour of the night made yellow by the stars. I hurried back to the ship where, having thrown off the black cloth with which I had cloaked myself for this expedition, I saw by the dim light of my lamp that my left elbow was no longer exactly like the rest of my body, but had taken on a slightly rough appearance like that of granite.

The day after this adventure I awoke with a mineral taste in my mouth and my eye-sockets torn by pains, like orbits lacerated by the circular ploughshares of their celestial bodies. The steamer forged ahead at full speed, and its smoke condensed with the breath of the giantesses to form big black clouds fringed with white, while a light, two-coloured snow fell softly on to the deck whenever a particularly strong wave shook the vessel and its tall mast, as if to bring down walnuts. Sitting on the wooden plaque which perhaps because we were nearing the Tropics had taken on the colour of mahogany, I observed in turn my stone-coloured elbow and the rigid column of space whose very rigidity made it too look like stone, a visual cylinder cut out of the sky by my porthole.

"Sitting on a rectangular plank cut into the shape of a raft which it seems I am to use as anything but a raft," I said to myself, "aboard a ship driven by women with magnificent hair whose every wave can avert a shipwreck, I measure the distance from my eye to that two-headed bird whose black plumage extends over the bounds of gestures triggered by the lure of terror. Having left behind a soft, cold land where my gaze had stuck fast (some sort of femininity seeming, I know not why, to be the cause of my departure), it was not until I had abandoned the asphalt with its sickly sweet stench that I became aware of my body and the word TORRID swooped down on my brain like a blazing beak, burying itself for ever in the humus of my head like a meteorite penetrating the earth and piercing it as if with a nail.

"Several psychological firebrands were burning black in my heart: there was the play of ideas, as absurd as sports when the striped jerseys of various colours confront each other on the great green field of Hope, that football game of cowards, whose goal invariably consists in placing the leather ball of being between the poles of reference which outline against the sky the parallelogram of eternal rest; there was the moral mime show, so perfectly badly staged that no actor will ever set the theatre alight with it; the bell of destiny which tires my ears with its endless nightmarish ringing; and finally the mushroom of duty, a fine shelter for families of insects, huddled together beneath this ridiculous umbrella which in their eyes has not even the merit of being poisonous. Side by side in the vast cage of my head there were numerous acclimatised species behind the bars of logic, and no untamed thought ever spoiled the show by leaping or crying out, domesticated as it was by its conditioned prison, the absence of all fasting and the putrid attentions of gaping onlookers. On Sundays and public holidays, specially marked on a calendar of misery and gall, the crowd would pour on to the streets, and while some drowned their sorrows in wine, that destroyer of melancholy (the only acceptable emotion on these days which are longer than Lent), others turned towards the zoological gardens which attracted them in the way that laws, bastions and prisons will always attract that filth known as 'decent folk'. More dutiful than excrement, the crowd stood for a long time watching the animals, making as if to run away whenever one of them made a show of anger, but immediately turning back again, reassured by the majestic bars. This vile mob was composed of none other than the champions of ideas, morals, vocations and duty, the builders of all kinds of fortresses which are nothing but enormous lavatories full of shrapnel, for whatever the projectiles that hit them, these projectiles will always have in common one characteristic, namely that they cover them in shit.[3] From time to time, however, sudden gusts of despair would threaten certain of the dwellings belonging to this crowd, and the walls would moan like suicide through the open mouths of their rubble stones. A lingering hubbub of drunken whores flowed out along the vast tree-lined avenues and in the silent gardens the boxwood lost its colour, sapped by the harsh rays of their cries and their clinging dust. The chambermaid in the clouds opened wide the gates of torment and there was nothing but rain, rain, rain and more rain…

"Artful little inhabitants, oh how you scurry back inside! Soon the water fell only on completely deserted streets, while you went to ground in your houses with their broken-down lifts, in your sitting-rooms with their fancy stuccoed ceilings whose plaster icing had long since contaminated your blood without your knowing it, so that it no longer ran red in your fine, plant-like veins but yellow, like dirty water in squalid pipes. 'The rainy season is here again,' you said, ignorant of the fact that this periodic return of the seasons was the regular tide which would one day put an end to your lives altogether, carrying them away when the very foundations of the tall, tranquil cliffs were finally eroded. Then what a curious sight! I do not think my cedar-wood plaque has ever recorded one more pure. The thrones of ash were swept away, the chess-boards jumbled up, the traditional marquetry of streets uprooted, all the bodies pulled from their cavities, the birds stripped of their wings so that flight in its perfectly pure state might exist of itself, without its prop of feathers and bones, the ravages of death spreading in all directions, stirring up the honey of all words and fermenting like alcohol in the huge hooped barrels of animal movements, at the hour when the sharpest points of skeletons project their whitish arrows into the night, purified by the metamorphoses of the wind. The monuments were razed to the ground, the pride of terraces pulled down to earth and only the grey pylons of distress pointed their uneven number of fingers to the sky…

"Decaying narcotic cities always procrastinating in the face of all greatness, despite the contemptible risk there is in building secret lakeside manor-houses on this shifting swamp, vomit of life whose every pore oozes the most vile secretions of tranquillity, swollen entrails of infants spread over the world like a mould, black slate of boredom on which the storms of the heart are never inscribed in letters of snow, inexhaustible bottle of misery sold by the litre for parsimonious intoxications, may you crumble to dust! Then above your glistening, rotting debris may the dawn open up the sky like a doorway through which its rays can circulate like blood. May it rise like a crystal postern in the sky painted blue by the sediment of our tears, this dawn of which the least I can say is that its charm is such that one day we shall have to make up our minds to break it too with our hands, this porcelain more delicate than that of a bowl of soup!"

Just as I pronounced these words I felt the wooden plaque I was sitting on give way beneath me, the boiler fires burned with a furiously intense heat and the giantesses, tossing their pale manes, sank together with the whole ship: we had arrived.

I have always found it more difficult than most to express myself other than by using the pronoun "I" — not that this should be seen as any particular sign of pride on my part, but because for me this word "I" epitomises the structure of the world. It is only in relation to myself and because I deign to pay them some attention that things exist. Should an object happen to appear which makes me aware of just how restricted the limits of my power really are, I stiffen into a mad rage and I invent Fate as if from the beginning of time it had been written that one day this object would appear on MY path, deriving its sole reason for being from this intrusion. Thus I walk in the midst of phenomena as if in the centre of an island which I trail along with me; the perspectives are solidified glances hanging from my eyes like those long filaments which the traveller collects inadvertently all over his body and carries with him — baggage of wispy lianas — when he crosses the tropical forest. I walk, and it is not I who change space but space itself which changes, moulded at the whim of my eyes which inject it with colours like arrows dipped in curare, so that it inevitably perishes as soon as my gaze has passed, a universe which I kill with marvellous pleasure, kicking away its colourless bones into the darkest depot of my memory. It is only in relation to myself that I am, and if I say "*it is raining*" or "*the sea is rough*," these are merely circumlocutions which convey that a part of me has resolved into fine droplets or that another part is swollen with dangerous eddies. The death of the world equals the death of myself. No disciple of any wretched religion will ever make me deny this equation, the only truth which dares aspire to my approval, although on the contrary I sometimes sense all the vague chastisements and monstrous threats which the word HE could hold for me.

So I will say that "I" had arrived, on My land, and that My rain fell incessantly; My fields of oats had lain flat beneath My gusts of wind and My sun shone like a sword, My sabre which "I" carried at My side. For here am I, sabre-rattling swashbuckler, prophet, pimp and many other men besides! Sabre-rattler of badly sharpened sentences which cut only a bevelled void instead of the heads I would like to see roll and collect in my basket; prophet, for I make a burlesque of prophesying and proclaiming woe; pimp of this world I profess to hate and which keeps me as its lover, until the day comes when it will throw me into the murky stream constantly flowing with old apple cores before being languorously swallowed up by the dry sand forming the sallow territories of death. For here I have come to cathedral Death, to this third person singular which a moment ago I crossed out with one stroke of my pen — Death, that grammatical pitchfork which imposes its ineluctable syntax on the world and on myself, that rule which makes all discourse nothing but a miserable mirage masking the nothingness of objects, whatever the words I utter and whatever this "I" which I put forward... All things considered, however, I prefer a bottle of whisky to these doctrinal reflections, for it is quite literally that I incorporate this alcohol, holding in solution millions of beings with their maximum potential.

I had arrived, then, and I was drinking whisky, just as I had done in the bar I described earlier. This liquor, you will tell me, is nothing but a crude grain alcohol, and only a thoroughly miserable ruffian would attach such great importance to this pathetic organic substance, whose most obvious property consists in transforming the field of consciousness into a vast communal graveyard. I will simply reply that my language, like all language, is figurative, and that for the word "whisky" you are quite at liberty to substitute any other term: absolute, murder, love, catastrophe or mandrake.

So I was drinking a bottle of absolute, a bottle of catastrophe, a bottle of mandrake... These words matter little to me, since any one of them represents my same eternal movement round an axis which I plant stupidly in the centre, like the pitiful flag placed at the Pole by a coloniser, who wants at all costs to see the liquid manure of his soporific little homeland flying in the form of coloured cloth on the great icy dome, where in fact the concept SLEEP is the only one black enough and frozen enough still to have any sort of meaning. These words — embryos of episodes and sentences — are of little importance, for what matters is that I myself am tossed between the cold and the burning heat, driven from one to the other like a bottle-imp and exposed to the little interstitial wiles of death, however strong the force of my disgust.

Here, however, on this island where I have just come ashore, the first person singular is no longer of prime importance and I must grant a voice to the dynamite of events.

# II.

Seated at a little table of plaited straw in the foyer of the most lavishly tasteless of hotels, a man was emptying a flask of whisky. From his white serge dinner-jacket it was plain for all to see that this scene was set in tropical parts. In fact, no sooner had he arrived in the country than he had hastened to replace the rainy garment, which would clothe him in the evenings in a carcass of dull coal, with a white outfit whose black lapels and trimmings delineated the contours obliterated by this pale colour, like the dark tracks left in the snow by a sledge which indicate to subsequent wayfarers the path to follow in this colourless ocean of solid foam. On the bottle standing in front of him the white label bearing the words "White Label" made perfectly clear what intense degree of whiteness the contents of this receptacle would allow one to attain, a whiteness composed negatively of a whole annihilated world, and positively of the floral patterns of frost settling on the walls of the vitrified brain like frail bones which would perhaps later be covered with new flesh.

The man was fairly tall with a tanned complexion, coarse hair and colourless eyes. His stiff movements seemed to be controlled by some secret geometry, and his lacquered feet were two plinths of black diamond. The flesh-coloured flower wilting in his buttonhole caused surprise, worn by this stone figure, like those batrachians found alive in certain Egyptian tombs where they had been immured for countless millennia! It was an enormous rose which opened like an explosion of words when gestures no longer suffice to demonstrate love and their physical framework therefore has to be extended into an imaginary framework of thoughts and words.

He wore no jewellery, but round his left wrist was a band of iron with no visible clasp, and thus permanently fastened to the base of his hand like the inflexible wheel of steel which governs the instincts, though often the fingers imagine themselves to be the architects. This iron band carried the rigidity of the figure to the extreme, a rigidity neither austere nor even severe like lead, but like those craggy ridges whose ribs extend horizontally beneath the sky in fixed directions, duplicated more softly by the clouds so that between object and reflection there is a certain play, as if to demonstrate that whatever the hardness of the reflected object, the image is always able to affect a sort of softness composed of freer lines and plant-like ramifications.

Sipping the liquid grain of his whisky, the man reflected upon his past (which he invented perhaps) and his memories swayed back and forth like ears of corn. He vaguely remembered having been born in a coastal town, and that it was to the waves' dried salt that he owed his stone-like appearance when, having plunged into their watery chaos, he would lie in the sun whose vertical rays caused faint white pyramids of salt crystal to appear here and there on his body, encasing it in armour such as his skeleton might have formed had it suddenly become external. It was this white garment of mourning which he still wore, the white mourning of surgical gowns so much more significant than black, since white is the colour of obliteration whereas black, far from being the colour of emptiness and nothingness, is much more the active shade which makes the deep and therefore dark substance of all things stand out, from the flight of despair whose magical blackness animates the blank parchment of the soul, to the supposedly sinister flight of the raven, whose croakings and cadaverous meals are but the joyful signs of physical metamorphoses, black as congealed blood or charred wood, but much less lugubrious than the deathly restfulness of white. Yet this desert whiteness did not rule out all subsequent possibilities, when it too would coagulate to form directions in the blood and when it too would know the three congruences of putrefaction.

The man in the white dinner-jacket, however, must have cared very little for this symbolism of colours, less colourful to him than the imagery of his memories which continued to rear up in his head like hairs standing on end in the grip of terror.

After that pale, hard beach whose grains of sand ran through his fingers like the delicate rosary beads he would tell as a small child, he had gone to live in a land full of mists, docks and mines where the women, all of whom were fair, were hollowed out like quarries, ripped open by the pickaxe of pleasure, flashing their eyes at all comers like efflorescences of ore. In sleazy taverns where the air laboriously trailed its old scraps of leather between four walls he had witnessed fatal brawls, and he recalled the disquieting little movement of the forefinger edging along the barrel of the gun when the gunman has no time to take aim and wants to fire an instant missile at his enemy, who is generally shielded by the seat of a chair, an overturned table or a prostitute's naked shoulder. These fights always ended in broken crockery and insults which piled up like heaps of coal on the dockside. It was from this country that the iron wrist-band came, and its colour evoked simultaneously the half-closed eyes of the women, the water of the river, the coal-dust and the bluish bruises which form whenever a punch, like a magic magnet, brings the true metal of decomposition to the body's surface.

A network of different professions made up the canvas on which this individual's woolly history was woven, a network that also created a multitude of relationships which cut across his life like ignoble assegais tipped as much with filth as with poison. One day he had rejected this loathsome professional net which normally constitutes the web of every life, no longer deigning to endure any enslavement other than that of the iron band, the hard, perfect circle which haunts the dark night of our minds, shining like the bluish steel of a rifle cocked ready for some unknown eternal hunt, in which we set the hounds of our desires upon a mysterious prey which flees in a circle round the maze of our forest, without our ever knowing (so swiftly does it move and so perfectly does it blend with the foliage) the exact nature of the relationship between pack, prey, huntsman and forest... It was the glimmering reflection of this chase that had planted the little speck of gold-dust right in the centre of his eye, like the glint in gamblers' eyes when the green baize is but a vast meadow across which they go hunting their luck, and when the bell tower marking the finish of this fearsome steeplechase tolls the fateful knell with its brazen heart, in order that the risky blood of suicide spill out like sound-waves in an endless ring. It was also the same hazy white glimmer he stared at, reflected in the convex glass of the bottle, above and below the label with the words "White Label", fixed there like a chalky cliff between a stormy sky and a howling sea.

Thus he had substituted for a treacherous net this metallic bracelet, this orb of lights glimpsed then solidified, and he wanted there to be no further question of that bailiff WORK in the civil structure of his life. He cast no more nets to catch the fish of the future and thought the beasts of the forest the only game worthy of him, because no preparation is necessary to kill them — a shot, after all, is so quickly fired! Likewise he had taken down all the sanitary notices displaying the moral code, and replaced them with a gleaming tubercular consumption caught on the zinc counters of bars where the most reviled drunken orgies took place.

These were the different ghostly elements which imbued the man in the white dinner-jacket with the extraordinary prestige I hinted at earlier. He stood in a room like a pivot, reducing furniture and bystanders alike to miserable little cogs designed solely to set him in motion, this man who was the axis of an enormous, completely unknown, mechanical eagle.

As I was saying, this room was lavish and utterly tasteless. The orchids bloomed in clusters of sweet stalactites and the sequinned velvet extended even to the black and white marquetry of the piano. Not far from a mahogany bar crammed with flasks and gleaming like the sides of a ship, a carpet of fur spread its manure of tactile sensations like taut springs seen from the inside. This was nausea in all its majestic beauty, nausea which without doubt constitutes man's one holy function, since it causes him to reject food, abandon the mask behind which he hoped to conceal his hideous face, turn as green as a hanged man and die more than a thousand deaths, a frantic fool who should be able to do nothing but vomit and vomit until he is dead.

The fact remains that in this excremental building, apart from the figure already described and a few specimens of the poorer class, there was a woman who was wonderfully pretty...

A man who goes to hunt animal furs in icy regions does not forget to take with him a nickel-plated flint lighter of the most delicate perfection to keep himself warm, and he values this lighter above all else, for he knows full well that should he find himself lost and far from all civilisation, he will need to make a fire in order to camp out in the snow, if he is not soon to become as stiff as a felled tree. This woman was that lighter. A clock which is about to strike midnight in the dry, purified air will only do so if its two hands, the large and the small, coincide with the vertical radius of the upper half of the clock-face. This woman was that coincidence. A metaphysical proposition is only valid if there is an absence of contradiction or if its contradictory terms are linked and reconciled. This woman was at the same time that absence and that link. When a bird of prey takes flight, it fixes its rounded eye like a menacing globe on an imaginary point in the sky towards which it soars in one straight burst of flight before swooping down on its prey, which is merely the earthly transposition of this point. This woman was that point and its transposition. In winter when the thaw begins, the ice on the rivers is broken up with pickaxes so the waters can carry away the enormous floes with minimal risk to shipping. This woman was that benevolent pickaxe which none the less hastens the debacle. When a peasant is afraid on stormy nights, he tells his rosary. This woman was that rosary. Rather than surrender to brutish policemen, the most admirable gangsters prefer to blow their brains out. This woman was the blood from these brains. One day a cloud of evil spells meets a hedgerow of pins. "How are you?" it asks. This woman was that mark of courtesy. A deceitful usurer was one day burned to death by order of the Inquisition. This woman was one of the flames which devoured him at the stake. Before mounting the scaffold, more than one revolutionary who had fallen victim to the Thermidorean reaction placed a last kiss upon a stranger's mouth. This woman was the flavour of that kiss. She was the richness and the flavour, the dryness, the fright and the torpor, the deceit of the Crusades and the American Civil War, the microscopic animal called SILENCE (though this is a notorious misnomer given that strictly speaking there is no such thing as silence), the vegetal whirl of evening gowns insufficiently luxurious to attempt to seduce a high-ranking officer, the freshness of forget-me-nots beneath a tree with eight branches and an extremely gnarled trunk covered in patches of green lichen, the unassailable result of fatal additions, the respect due to papal decisions, the Q.E.D. concluding theorems, the hint of freedom occasionally glimpsed in the degree of approximation of a scientific law, the handkerchief which holds the entire luggage of an emigrant, the ash which is nothing but the deposit left by the hearth — she was all these things, and the spiral of her hair united these contradictory terms, carried off by a dialectical wind towards the very corner of the room at which the petrified man directed his gaze.

As soon as he noticed the woman, this man paid no more attention to the bottle. The whisky was engulfed in the maelstrom of the past which was itself immediately reabsorbed, and few ripples on the surface signalled its disappearance. Sparrow-hawks flocked from the four corners of the room, hovering for a moment around the central chandelier which shattered suddenly, showering the assembled guests with fragments of candle-ring and lumps of burning wax. Only a brothel lamp continued to burn, its flaming hand lighting up the intimate secrets of the scene about to take place, and it was by this one sensual light that the man in the white dinner-jacket suddenly seized the bottle and hurled it through the window into the void outside, where it shattered on the flagstones with a loud crash of broken glass.

Panic-stricken, all the diners fled, leaving the man in the white dinner-jacket and the blonde woman face to face, more alone than on a raft when one by one all their companions have drowned, so that apart from the surviving couple all that remains on the pile of rotten planks is thirst, hunger, anguish, the storm and love born of fear.

Then, in this atmosphere devoid of all humidity and of the dense mists of humanity, free from the gamut of colours and the latent, though non-existent opposition between white death and black death, the blonde woman and the white man fell into each other's arms and made love.

Pessimism is a towering skyscraper eighty storeys high in the suburbs of the soul at the end of a long avenue with waste ground on either side and a few poorly stocked little shops. Several ultra-fast staircases give access to the building, running up from the cellars to the roof-gardens. The comfort of this place leaves nothing to be desired and only the greatest luxury is acceptable, but every Friday the residents gather on the ground floor to read from a bible bound in the skin of a blind man. The psalmic words they intone rise up through the pipes, sigh in the stoves and sweep the chimneys coated inside with a black grease which leaves dirt on the skin. Water runs constantly in the bathrooms and showers beat down on the numbed bodies, peppering them with sand. On Sundays the bed linen unrolls by itself and nobody makes love. For this tower block, like an obscene phallus scraping the vulva of the sky, is usually a hive of sexual activity. The most beautiful woman of all lives there, but no one has ever known her. It is said that, dressed in furs and feathers, she keeps herself shut away in a first-floor apartment as if in a white safe. Her windows are scissors which cut short both shadow and breath. Her name is AURORA.

High up amidst the loftiest terraces of this building, the white man and the blonde woman made love. A single smoky flame was all that still burned in the chandelier, and the men had returned to their meagre cages where they were prisoners of their hats, clothes and identity papers. Up and down the walls of the hotel, rustling noises could be heard as if they were infested by a swarm of tiny insects, while in a remote bedroom, water oozed from the taps drop by drop, a straight, watery line which could never close up to make a neck-chain. Far away in the countryside a dog was barking, but his howls could force open no door save that of the ear, whose shell-like aperture let in the sound of their echo. From the depths of the most distant islands, where the sob of the forest merges with the opacity of its colour, a murmuring arose and a thousand voices mingled their amorous lines like the diamonds of mysterious burglars on a pane of glass.

"In whatever country we might be," these voices were saying, "to whatever frontiers we might have been driven by hunger, thirst and their acid storms, it is always the same gust of sand which dries out our faces like parchment. Stray lightning slips through the undergrowth; it eliminates our shadows, lighting us up from head to foot. Above the obstacle put in our way by these tangled lianas are the bottomless precipices of the air, the torrential storms and the mines of gold which amass to form the sun. Which trapper setting out from the most dismal suburbs of a European city will succeed in capturing this gold, whose bars are battering-rams for beating against prison walls? Which explorer will succeed in discovering this wonderful hair with a curl that is the one true image of gushing springs, vegetal death and the wheelings of a bird of passion?"

Then the voices dispersed like mist at the stealthy approach of noon, all the mirages vanished and the couple were left lying in the emptiness, out of the paths of the wind and the dark arrows of direction. Their hearts swelled gradually like two waves laden with seaweed, but soon they were shipwrecked and were nothing but a single one of your bottles bobbing up and down on its own huge waves far from sextants, meridians and declinations.

Thus, until cock-crow the white man and the blonde woman made the secret spirit-level tremble with their caresses. Then, at daybreak, they fled on horseback into the reconstructed universe.

The towns they visited were all alike. There were always industrial streets, gardens and squares arranged round anonymous statues. The houses were piles of sad concrete and the windows at the top of these buildings directed their eternally weary gaze upon the bituminous roads whose surface no sun was ever strong enough to crack. There were always crimes which no fear of police power was capable of holding in check, and behind the shutters were creatures who ate, drank and made love heedless of the life of the stones and the strange possibilities promised by the perspectives of the road. There were many vagabonds roaming the streets, but not one had a stare that was powerful enough to bring the buildings and monuments tumbling down on top of one another. The women blinked their worn-out eyelids like shabby old slippers knocked against each other in winter for warmth. The back-street abortionists were always out of work, for not a single train of souls escaped the world before being pompously set in the honesty, filth and sticky compost of longevity. In the museums every room yawned silently, the markets traded while in the harbours the ships languished, for all that remained to swallow them up was an ever-identical horizon, since all the powers of dreams and the torments of the imagination were concentrated in two individuals.

The white man and the blonde woman rode through every country mounted on two pinkish-coloured horses. They swam the seas and their horses' manes added to the frothing of the foam, while their breasts became muscular shields able to withstand the onslaught of the waves hurled at them like a spray of stone slabs.

The North Pole had revealed itself in all its cold nakedness like a drowned princess, and the icebergs were adrift, gliding along like huge gems detached from the ears which had worn them and lost in the deep blue velvet of a boundless salt-water jewel case. The South Pole was more obscure, remaining shrouded in misty veils, an unknown captive thrown into an icy circus-ring and exposed to the taunts of the stars and the ferocity of polar bears. The Equator let the ends of its belt hang down carelessly and the Earth itself almost let fall its maritime gown to reveal its brown flesh scarred by fires. The equinoxes came round one after the other like rings of dancing maidens whose feet soon roughen the grass, strange songs wound themselves round the tropical poles and the compass needles jumped about like crickets. The five parts of the world stretched out like the fingers of a hand whose palm the two riders explored, seeking to discover the major line of their destiny in the furrows of its rivers and valleys.

This line, the exact trace of which they were never able consciously to distinguish, was extremely sinuous, twisting and turning more often than a hair at the mercy of atmospheric variations. Here and there statues rose up, human milestones whose sudden solidified leaps defied the sky with its jaw of blue alcohol which sought to eat into their pale forms, and the most luminous glaciers (those that fish their white scales from the very depths where stars shine like octopuses) shot their frosty arrows in a vertical direction to indicate the one route which could have shortened their journey. However, neither of the travellers heeded these warning signs, and all external organisms went unnoticed by them.

Boredom, though, which can undermine the proudest of fortresses and penetrate towns protected by drawbridges, slipping through their keyholes without a key — boredom was to be the corpuscular sphere which would pierce the limpid walls of their eyes and sit like a dead sun at the zenith of their world of passion.

We do not come into the world with impunity, and there is no possible escape. Though the wandering couple passed through the spaces between objects like a comet, a perfectly closed universe contained between the meeting of their mouths and the joining of their genitals, still their organs were not so hermetically sealed that there was no room for a tiny crack large enough to allow boredom to seep in. This boredom, being the envoy of external objects, came to bring back into their weighty web this celestial body made of the flesh of two beings which a bloody kiss had momentarily freed from the pull of gravity.

The horses grew sad, and now their hooves made only a very slow, monotonous sound just like the noise of carriages passing through towns on cold nights when the streets are muddy and the listener is nagged by insomnia. The lovers exchanged mournful glances and had just enough strength to smile at each other as they saw the seasons collapsing before them like old rags. Boredom reigned supreme on the battlefield, and the defeated couple could only retreat in a straight or broken line through the half-melted snow mixed with earth, a brownish amalgam which would henceforth constitute the only ground their horses would trample.

However, love did not bow its head, still keeping aloft its crest of amber and foam, and

like a corpse to its shroud,
like a table to its trestles,
like a glacier to its mountain,
like a river to its valley,
like a surface to its area,
like a furrow to its plough,
like a bird to its flight,

like a sea to its tide,
like a flame to its light,
like a mouth to its bite,
like a witch to her stake,
like a liquor to its savour,
like a bourgeois to his stupidity,
like a soldier to his cowardice,
like form to its matter,
like a facet to its crystal,
like a tongue to its kiss,
    like music,
    like misery,
        a pang of hunger,
        an idea,
        a pit,
        a ravine,
        a sceptre,
        a steeple,
the blonde woman and her lover (fine examples of the melancholy perseverance of bones through the yellow groves and snake-like entrails of boredom) were still bound to each other.

Meanwhile, however (links at varying distances prolonging the torment of this chain), several dead cities raised their fists of ash toward the sky, birds nested in their ruins and despite the corrosive rain which made necks and faces hollow, the two parallel mouths fled through a space inadequately defined by this present love, along river-banks loaded with goods in transit by the docks of time.

Beneath this decisive blade of steel, lips grew thinner and increasingly white as pleasure melted away ever more quickly, and there was no question of stemming this leak of colours with any sort of construction, be it an abstract scaffolding of stars or the mortar of stagnant gravity. In the necropolises, tombs were shorn like flocks of sheep by the rays of the sun, so that the tapestries of memory might be woven from this mossy wool, while the transparent corpses were threaded with filigree, metaphysical diagrams rather than arteries or bones.

From this frail line — the very line of fate which the couple in search of their destiny unknowingly followed — hung everything: the two opposite extremes like the pans of a pair of scales, the brick alignment of identity, the dormitory beneath the rafters of the damp school of the dogmatic, where the beds are all alike though occupied by bodies each slightly different, the furniture which evokes death more surely than any clock, the spiteful jackals snarling at the hair-cloth tent of the harbinger HAPPINESS, the heart, that sovereign pyramid in a desert of blood, the bitterness of divine herbs fed on substances released by flesh and bone, the letter with a red seal signed by a hidden vampire that bites into the white spaces between the lines, the machine-gun with human bullets and cartridges called *Desires*, the prehistoric ages uncovered by cutting into the deposits of unhappiness, the unconscious arrow which searches as it flies for the direction it has already found from the start, the tip of its feverish head drawing ever nearer to its target at catastrophic speed, the sexual organs which join together but do not merge, like liquids of different densities, the blind meteor whose eyes illuminate, the looking-glass which cracks beneath the weight of superstitious fears unless it adorns itself with superficial wounds when rings bite into it, the love which struggles eternally against boredom just as the colour red struggles against the grey of foggy winter skies, the submersion of plumblines into the depths of an ocean calmer than vegetation, mortal manure destined to become fertiliser, death's flatterers, those courtiers who carry metaphysical canes and verbose ribbons, the heavy flight of birds weary of all migration and confined to the dried-up tree whose branches are no longer any protection against death, post offices where stamps are cancelled and thus daily put to death, the desperate water mains which forbid the taps from stopping up on pain of death, the two pylons of unequal height which mark the entrance to the avenues of death and lastly the fine displays of light, fireworks of deception, gold dentures on the gums of nothingness.

Such a series of objects, tiered like waves at high tide, must of necessity be followed by another representing, as it were, the low tide. That is why suddenly there appeared: the warm streets which are the true arteries of a city because the red corpuscles of carnal delights thread their way through them, the daintiness of a woman's foot, as fascinated by the gleaming leather in which it is trapped as a lark lured by a sparkling mirror, the laughter which pierces the air like a corkscrew in order to decant its wine for an abject feast, the hidden life of frenetic intestines and the pendulum of tears beneath the dome of a vagina. All these different stems, however, merged to form a single field and suddenly, beneath a harsh sky of flawless blue, the white man and the blonde woman, freed from the snowy slough in which they had been lost for centuries, could be seen galloping beside ploughed strips of land, clearing streams and hedges and advancing towards a mysterious point on the horizon to which they were unfailingly drawn as the future scene of a fresh embrace.

On the edge of a vast sandy desert, not far from the luxury hotel where the first waves of this story begin to rise, stands a gigantic penal colony in the shape of a cone truncated very close to its tip.

The prison cells are spaced out along a spiral gallery; the highest, reserved for those condemned to death, have but one tiny window on to the inside, so that the prisoners may gaze directly down into the well formed by the middle of the cone, a hollow cylinder into which, as noon strikes, the sun's rays fall vertically and stand upright like weapons in a rack. Below are the dwellings occupied by the gaolers, but contrary to what one would expect, the latter are not in the least concerned that above their heads is a whole spiral of curses resulting from these two connected causes: the spiral layout of the cells and the rebellion inherent in the sinister condition of the prisoner.

All around the cone is an expanse of sand corrugated by small dunes whose form is not spiral like the prison but sinusoidal. Only the swirling wind corresponds to the geometry of the cells and sometimes it rushes in, appropriately coil-shaped, with a hissing of snakes.

The desert is a rose garden whose petals have fallen through the fingers of that bad yellow gardener whose rake is made of scorching rays. Today an invisible schoolmaster is the overlord of this expanse, and the espaliers which imprison the roses have turned into staircases. Day and night, a certain number of convicts move around the spiral singing songs which are never anything but dismal lessons:

*Declension:*[4]

| | |
|---|---|
| Nominative | *moi* |
| Genitive | *mythe* |
| Dative | *mie* |
| Vocative | *merde!* |
| Accusative | *mue* |
| Ablative | *mort* |

| *Conjugation:* | |
|---|---|
| Present indicative | *je mords* |
| Imperfect " | *je murais* |
| Perfect " | *je m'ourdis* |
| Future " | *je m'ordonnerai* |
| Conditional | *je muserais* |
| Subjunctive | *que je m'use* |
| Supine | *mortel* |
| Gerund | *amour* |

When the riders reached the foot of this prison the voices of the convicts fell silent and the cone began to turn on the spot, slowly at first, then very quickly.

Once it had reached full and regular speed, it began to rock on its base and then suddenly toppled right over and sank into the ground, dragging with it gaolers, convicts and conjugations in its hidden spiralling folds. They were not to disappear entirely, however, or at least their disappearance was to be marked by certain lasting signs; consequently four long furrows appeared, each coming from one of the cardinal points and soon joining up at the medial point in the figure of a cross on the ground, at the place where the prison inmates must now have been leading a subterranean life reduced to a mere reflection. At the same time the two pink horses were divesting themselves of their fleshly frames, and soon they were no more than a pair of extremely grubby skeletons, each with a rusty bit in its mouth.

Thus the white man and the blonde woman found themselves standing on the ground, the differently pointed tips of their shoes in a row in the same straight line which ran parallel to one of the arms of the cross. Their mouths, parched after such a long, hard journey, were now merely two fossilised birds trapped in the air that was hard like coal, a vein of love the full length of which they had explored without managing to extract anything but a metal fit for dream-like crystallisations. Their fingers, in four separate groups, stretched out almost vertically towards the ground and their gaze, perpendicular to this cluster of digital lines, flew towards the most distant zone of the horizon as if to overcome the rigid ascendancy of one geometry by means of another, this latter a geometry without limits.

A short distance from the intersection of the two arms of the cross could be seen the pieces of a broken bottle, heavier shards mixed in with the fine sandy fragments of the shattered rose garden. As soon as the man noticed them, he broke the geometric order in which his fingers, feet and body had been arranged, walked towards these pieces of glass and, picking them up, attached them to the iron band from which, with one violent movement, he had managed to free his wrist. Holding these different objects in his left hand he walked to the point where the furrows met and, plunging his arm as deep as he could into the sand, he buried them at the centre of the cross and then returned to stand beside the blonde woman. Now, however, he noticed that his left arm was no longer supple as before but appeared white, hard and bare like the stone arm of a statue. It was then that, the blonde woman having asked him his name, he put the same question to her and she replied "Aurora."

The voice which uttered this name was as husky and fresh as its three syllables, and the word AURORA stretched out, soft and pure like the desert.

Once the prison was swallowed up the reddish earth had turned to colourless dust and a cross was now all that stood out against the uniform surface of the sand. Aurora spoke, and as if they partook of the substance of her name, each one of her words caused a tiny particle of the desert to stir and alter the shape of the cross. As Aurora made her way through the labyrinth of sentences in which she was her own Ariadne, guided by the meaningful thread of her breathing, the medial point actually rose up, possibly under the hidden pressure of the prison spiral attempting to resurface in order to hear Aurora. Drawn upwards by this movement, the four furrows remained joined to the medial point and, their points of origin none the less retaining their original and cardinal immobility, they gradually became the slanting edges of a pyramid whose apex rose ever higher and would certainly have turned into the quadrangular blade of a dagger had Aurora continued to speak for very much longer.

"The delicacy of honey is a colour softer than the patina of time," said Aurora, who with dilated pupils absent-mindedly watched the pyramid grow. "When roads stretch out beneath the traveller's footsteps like slaughtered animals and when fever, fallen from the treetops, is but a little liquid bell suited to the often ungainly dance of the head, the bones of the dead climb their crematory slopes, and with a red-hot iron the scorching fires of oblivion efface the tattoos on their skulls, those bluish drawings more defiling than graffiti on the limbs of statues. In the ravine where the earth burns your old straw forms, O dead ones, when the amalgam of blood, fear and pain forming the seal on your passports turns to liquid in the hands of strange ambassadors, the pyramid comes to rest, more simply than thunder or the cry of an Egyptian jackal! The embalmers' circular movement as they wrap bodies in bandages, the flight of kites which extend to the air itself the circular shape of the highest turrets, the work of ploughshares when the wooden furniture splits and gives way beneath its ghostly burden, the gleaming metal of diverse forestry developments, the grinder's stupid wheel which will never sharpen the real knife of murderers — all these external biting actions of more or less acceptable value melt in my own mouth without cutting into it, from the moment the pyramid of Egypt towers like an anti-sky, a heap of solid space and overturned stars. The word TEMPEST riddles my cheeks with a hail of pinpricks. My bosom glistens like a fish. I dry out the sweat of time with the swirling air of my fan *Space*. I behead the kings of direction on the block of *Time*. A pharaoh dressed in red brandishes his axe, the sovereign of fornication. In graveyards the wind takes flight like a bird with an enormous wingspan, rushing across human frontiers all of which are more stupid than posts used as road signs, as stakes for torture, or for executions. May the lightning crumble and scatter its electric pollen over the least putrid flanks, if the marshalling yards do not assemble the cattle of nations, little pepperpots with no flavour and oh so little spice! A boundless blue sky bursts through in the North but the North, carved in dirty white wood, is little better than a mechanical harvester. I listen to the rational clamour of the leaves in the woods, but I much prefer the sweet song of the railways. One day a child who had not yet killed either mother or father gave me a cross of repentance. In response I gave him a coffin door. His penis rose up like the "stop" signal on a goods railway; I drew it gently on to the turntable of my breast. Then he began to moan, and each of his cries engendered three toads which immediately started jumping and which, stickier than constellations, are still jumping in eternity. The heavens had tipped their mine of stars on to my head, so I attacked the black sky, changing it into a glacier simply by kicking it with my pale toes. I am the Leaf and I am everything, but above all I am *serious* and my loveliest pendant earrings are pendulums of gravity. The glass pendants swinging from the hems of *haute couture* gowns are but the harbingers of my destiny, crystal signals, alarm sirens fashioned from the foam of the waves when the shadowy tribe of the drowned embarks on its distant migrations, under the sea like everything which genuinely constitutes the Serious. I burst into laughter at the sight of this pyramid my misty eyes are only just beginning to discern, and I stretch out at full length along this concrete sand marked with small ridges like the weals on a criminal beaten at the Place de Grève.[5] Loquacious world armature of amphorae. A double valley ripens the imaginary caress of my serious thighs…"

Aurora was silent for a moment, but turning to look at her companion with eyes streaked with layers of dark red, in a thin but rasping voice like the line of black ink describing the progress of an earthquake on a seismograph's white sheet of paper, she began to sing the following ballad which she accompanied with gentle hip movements, lifting alternate hands up to her hair, as yellow as the straw of a rustic resting-place:

The brothers' house with the basement window
halfway up the hill between crates and palm trees
is not to blame for the parallel tracks
of the railway whose carriages are baskets

A bung in a barrel of ghosts
all marinated in old wine
is released to disturb in their homes
those still with faith in the Lord

A desert as dry as the sediment of alcohol
scorched by the candles of gall
fulminates if the sand decomposes
powder of ossicles powder of honey

Mountain of transient reasons
its winding passes like a ship's propeller
its peaks are icy turbines which clasp
the vapour of sobs in their frozen white arms

An eagle a plesiosaurus a cross
too many insects walled up in the workings
erode the wooden feet of kings' thrones
polished by the wax of ages.[6]

For a moment the silence re-formed its heavy oil-slick conducive to countless hidden combustions, but soon there came shouts from the pyramid which lit the powder keg. Was this perhaps the prison convicts massacring their gaolers and then tearing one another to pieces, seized by a sudden frenzy of mass murder and hoping the morose acridity of their blood would have the strength to wear away the huge stones that formed the flesh of their new prison?

Within a fairly wide radius of the pyramid slight disturbances began to trouble the surface of the sand and one by one limbs appeared, at first running with blood, then hard and clean like polished pieces of marble. Various birds cut through the air with their razor-sharp wings, and vast panoramic back-cloths then appeared — scenery set up for a final act which would surely end in the only satisfactory way possible, that is, in a river of blood.

Meanwhile Aurora seemed to have forgotten the man standing beside her as stiff as a mummy, wrapped in all the earthly bandages from which, for a time, he had thought himself freed. Aurora had eyes only for the tip of the pyramid, and even the point of intersection of its four edges could not rival the sharpness of her gaze.

There was no way of foreseeing when this situation would change. The pyramid remained motionless in the night which had now fallen, a huge heap of coal piled up in the warehouses of past and future, on the banks of that invisible river along which trade is conducted between the rational regions on the one hand and the distant lands on the other, which from time to time send their colourless vessels full of bitter produce and wares spiced with anguish. The geometric sky reflected innumerable polyhedra of which only the sharpest bones were visible, pale points as if made of chalk. A tangible eternity lent a metallic hardness to the atmosphere and the scattered sections of body became ever more numerous, transforming the desert into a wide ghostly field full of flowers of dust and broken statues.

When the last convict's cry had made itself heard along with the feeble flow of his last few drops of blood, Aurora abandoned her companion who seemed once more to have turned to stone, this time for good, and walked straight to the foot of the pyramid. She then began slowly to climb up, using hands which no human toil had until then deflowered.

Reaching the top she stripped naked and parted her legs in such a way that the pyramid became a sort of stake upon which she was impaled, one of her legs in line with the North edge of the pyramid, the other leg with its South edge and her vulva touching the apex which scratched it with its stone finger-nail. Her loose hair flowed above her, the only living wave in this desolate world. The wind, which had encountered no obstacle in the desert, advanced violently, and its jagged blade made Aurora's body spin round, a sorry weather-vane at the mercy of this tyrant's sadistic will.

With each turn of Aurora around the axis of the pyramid a little more of her body was torn to shreds and the pyramid turned red with blood, first at its peak and then further and further down as Aurora grew weaker, a slave to the sensuality of the wind.

The whole of the upper half of the pyramid was now coloured red, and only Aurora's head remained in place on the top, a new sphinx whose body might seemingly have been imprisoned inside the mass of stone which in fact was only its plinth.

Aurora's eyes had closed with languor but her hair, the last conscious part of her, still flowed freely, coiling more seductively than a snake.

When the pyramid was red from top to bottom, the wind suddenly dropped. At the summit Aurora's hair still hoisted its diffuse crest, a red vapour rising from the crater of a volcano, but already an underground rumbling began to shake the whole desert and the stars grew dim.

Suddenly a cry rang out. It was the mummified man, who was being swallowed up by the sand as all the marble limbs disappeared.

Then Aurora's hair became a mass of swirling flames and in a flash the most remote comets hastened to add their incandescent hair to the white heat of this furnace, while the pyramid lost its shape and was suddenly of earth. A moment later it was but a monstrous volcano and, in a flow of lava which would reduce the entire desert to ashes more effectively than the sun, it spat out the mutilated entrails and bits of chain from the corpses of those who had been its prisoners.

# III.

The volcano which had formed as Aurora's hair came into contact with the top of the pyramid (her whole body having just been worn away by this four-edged file) had scarcely ceased erupting, its lava and scoria scarcely cooled down, confining innumerable insects in a prison of gangue, when, in the very direction the feet must once have pointed in that belonged to the dried-up corpse for which such an Egyptian pyramid served as a mausoleum, there appeared a ship, at first a minute vertical line on the horizon, but which soon grew large enough to fill the entire landscape. A white flag flew at the stern and on it was painted the following rainbow-coloured inscription:

α and ω

Lamartine said:

*It was from the ashes of the dead that the Fatherland was created.*

Make certain you are all shod with the skin of your ancestors, then you will always be sure to *carry your fatherland with you on the soles of your shoes.*

Q.E.D.

A young man wearing fawn leather buskins and with his left arm in a sling was asleep in the middle of the deck, lying with his face turned towards the sky, stretched out on a rough wooden plank which raised him a few inches from the deck. The ship advanced in a direction perpendicular to the movement of the sun, as if it wanted to slice with its mast through the trajectory of the star, causing it to drop into the sea like a fruit whose curved stalk has just been cut. Between each of the scales in the air that was burning none the less, the memory of Aurora coiled like the white snake which inhabits the coldest crevasses of polar regions. Apart from the sleeping passenger not a living soul appeared to be on board, but the boat was obviously driven by some secret mechanism, for despite the calm which left its sails hanging creased like an old woman's cheeks, it progressed steadily, trailing behind it a wake which made it resemble a philosophical meditation on the sequence of historical causes.

When night fell the ship maintained its course, sailing across the entire expanse of the enormous echoing cave where stars hang like stalactites, until it reached the first basement window of unbarred daylight. Then, finding itself in a little creek, the ship came to a stop; the young man disembarked, stepped ashore as if he were sleepwalking, lay down along the border between soil and sand and continued his slumber, while the enigmatic vessel resumed its course, this time with its sails billowing and its mast pointing like a finger towards the sky that was turning a vile shade of blue.

When the sleeping man awoke it was low tide. The sea had receded, leaving the bottom of the creek fully exposed, and it was easy to see from what vestiges remained that a most important temple had once stood there. As the young man explored these ruins, however, he noticed that besides the broken colonnades and the loose squares of stone lying on the ground amongst the coral and the algae, there were various objects whose presence was puzzling, for he could find no reason for their being in such a place. There was an enormous shell with a single valve split lengthways (a shell which, judging by its visibly planned central position, had been in place since the time of the temple and not subsequently washed up by the sea) and several tools half eaten by rust: two spades, two picks, two long saws of pliable metal, a butcher's hook and two pieces of metal in the shape of spearheads.

The young man was wondering to what use these instruments might have been put and what cataclysm at sea had wrecked the temple, when he noticed between the site of this edifice and the boundary to which the sea had receded the remains of a strongly built sea wall, no doubt in the past employed to prevent the sea from flooding the creek at high tide and thus protecting the temple against the waves which should otherwise have engulfed it. In the event of enemy invasion this wall was probably systematically destroyed, the sea then becoming an unassailable guardian of the sacred objects. The temple's provident builder must have reasoned thus, thinking of everything except the low tide. That is why the young man — who had just made these rapid deductions — driven at once by his curiosity and his greed for gold, resolved to explore the temple ruins in minute detail in order to see if there was not some hidden treasure to be discovered there.

Vexed after a long but fruitless search, the character in detective's buskins was about to leave the creek when he noticed that the central shell was not absolutely stable and that the light touch of one finger was all that was needed to make it rock. Pushing a little harder with both hands (having first carelessly undone the sling supporting his left arm) he managed to roll the shell over, and he then saw that its underside concealed the entrance to an underground chamber. Although this cavity was completely flooded, the explorer did not hesitate to go in.

Forced to hurry in order to finish his search before running out of breath, he was already preparing to come back up into the open air after having found nothing when, running the palm of his hand along one of the walls, he felt something metallic. He promptly seized the object he had come into contact with and, easily dislodging it from the jaws of the crack in which it had previously been caught, with a thrust of his legs he returned to the surface.

Then the diver sat on a section of column and set about identifying his booty. Carefully removing the grass and tiny shells that covered it, he saw that the object he had thought precious, imagining it to be part of a treasure-trove, was in fact merely a rectangular plaque of sheet metal, albeit engraved with a vast number of characters which, although practically worn away, were still legible. After much painstaking research (abandoned several times then desperately resumed almost straight away), the young man in the fawn leather buskins managed more or less to piece together the following text:

"On this day, 25th corona in the 800th year of Corpuscular Dusk, I, DAMOCLES SIRIEL, High Priest of this temple, bequeath my story to mankind, not that I attach any great importance to posterity but because I have always been naturally inclined to exhibitionism.

Twenty-eighth and last of the dynasty of Hierarchs, before abandoning this sanctuary soon to be engulfed by the sea (leaving in the frail barque to whose nautical capacities I have entrusted my bones and my fate), I leave this sheet of corrugated iron between two stones of the subterranean womb, the key to which I alone possessed, and on this metal plaque I have personally inscribed the story of my life up to the final catastrophe which marks its close.

I was always cruel, even as a child. I hated all men (pathetic creatures barely fit for mating) as well as all beasts and plants, my only feelings of affection being reserved for inanimate objects. The sight of a bearded face sent me into a fit of rage. The only thing I liked about women was their crystal jewellery. When I saw them naked, in order to arouse my desire I had to imagine that they were statues — cold, hard beings without viscera or skin — and not the female variety of those sinuous little goatskin bottles, full of sobs and ill-defined sensations, called *men*. Even my own body I regarded with pure disgust and made use of any substance capable of giving it the appearance of granite, often remaining motionless for hours on end in the belief that this would to some extent enable me to become more like a statue. It was only at the close of day, at the hour when most men return to their cells for a loathsome sleep or to indulge in the paltry pleasure which perpetuates the species, it was only when the sun's rays ceased to warm this rabble that a new flow of vigour would run through my limbs and for me life would really begin.

Leaving the family home through a hole in the wall I had made with my nails, I would wander for hours in the countryside and across the barren plains contemplating the stars, those beautiful gems whose cold brilliance filled me with delight. I would study closely their various colours, grouping them in infinite combinations in my mind, but most of all I liked to imagine (and this was the main theme of my meditations) that one day perhaps they would turn into so many meteors and fall, crushing the Earth beneath an avalanche of rocks, thereby obliterating every human blemish from the face of the globe. I felt no hatred, however, for the Earth itself, that platform on which my feet stood, for I regarded it as another star. At very most I might have reproached it for not allowing me to admire it in all its spherical splendour, but I hoped that the end of the world would detonate its incendiary torpedoes as soon as possible, for these alone would be capable of annihilating the entire human race.

The rare members of this species who saw me pass (I say "rare" owing to the late hour at which I took these strolls and also to the fact that everyone drew back from my path since the day I had pelted the small band of friends I had had in my youth with pieces of flint, imagining that I would strike from their bodies not putrid blood, but sparks capable of igniting the sky), these few beings who met me on my nocturnal rambles instinctively began to tremble just as if they had seen a poisonous snake at the mere sight of my stiff gait and movements which seemed hampered by a ton weight of rock. They were not unaware of my loathing for them, with their imprecise curves and their unverifiable, momentary sweats, because I cared only for rocks, the perspectives of buildings, the stars and the surface of the Earth: vast, bare and perfectly even when devoid of all irregularities.

At this point I must tell you that for me life has always been synonymous with everything soft, lukewarm and undefined. Liking only the intangible, that which is no part of life, I arbitrarily identified all that is cold, hard or geometric with this constant, and it is for this reason that I love the angular lines the eye casts into the sky to apprehend the constellations, the mysteriously premeditated order of a monument and finally the ground itself, the most perfect plane locus of all figures.

Let no one imagine though that this timeless love of the cold and the immutable, as well as of geometric forms, corresponds in any way to even the slightest taste for order and intelligence. For the truth is that I despise both these human excretions, and if I am attracted to some building or geometrical figure, then this has nothing to do with the intrinsic fact of its being in proportion, but simply because this proportion gives me the illusion that it will last for ever.

Day and night death hung over me like a mournful threat. Perhaps I strove to convince myself that this minerality would enable me to elude it, forming some sort of armour, and also a hiding-place away from death's shifting but infallible attacks (rather like what insects make out of their own bodies when they feign death in order to ward off danger). Fearing death, I loathed life (since its crowning achievement is inevitably death) — hence my horror of all those monstrous human beings from whom I was descended and who, being monsters themselves, never ceased giving birth to yet more monsters, because any being, starting with myself, whose life consists in waiting for death can be nothing other than a monster.

When I dreamed, it was generally of desolate avenues lined with metal scaffolding or else of horses reduced to their mechanical elements, but sometimes also of living women with white skin whose lips I would bite... For biting is the only part of kissing I have ever understood (even if I appear to speak of it in gentle terms), because to me flesh only seems worth caressing on the one condition that it be simultaneously devoured. Thus my idea of love was always associated with this image of hardness, and ever since this time I have considered my mouth, with its cold scree of teeth, to be more than any other the organ intended for love.

As I have said, in my youth I contented myself with striking my friends till I drew blood, tearing plants out of the ground, torturing animals and also raping one or two girls upon whom I chanced, when I considered their bodies sufficiently hard and whitened by the dust of the road or else bronzed by the rays of the sun for me to believe that these were not earthly creatures but unhuman idols. Having satisfied my desire I would run off, knowing that not one of them would dare tell what had happened for fear of my revenge, and smiling at the thought that each one bore the mark of my jaw on some part of her flesh in the form of a bite. At this unsettled age, however, I had not yet realised my potential genius.

When my father died, I inherited his high rank. I was solemnly dressed in a white silk corset with two stiffened pouches and a scarlet toque (the object of which was to make me look like the male organ of virility), and thus invested with these derisory insignia of my new status, I became the High Priest. At first I was extremely displeased, thinking that this office would curb my freedom, but soon, on the contrary, I was delighted when on reflection (for this idea had not occurred to me straight away), I realised that the title of Hierarch would give me complete immunity, and consequently I would be able to satisfy my wildest desires without the slightest fear of punishment.

I had at my disposal a large number of women who were slaves in the service of the temple and obliged to obey my every command on pain of death. I was also assured of their silence, for they lived a cloistered life and for the most part were even chosen because they were mute. Moreover, when it came to purely sensual excesses, anything I might do would remain of little consequence, the people being accustomed to the periodic orgies required by their religion and therefore unlikely to be scandalised by the knowledge that similar events were taking place in my palace. Furthermore, did not my new role (which as I have just said rendered me invulnerable, so to speak) already constitute the best possible shield?

First of all, therefore, I had three rooms of the palace converted for my singular pleasures. In the first room there was a block of ice, in the second a number of whips and razors and in the third, which was entirely of marble, there was nothing at all. The women I had singled out from amongst the priestesses were brought into the first room. I had to find out whether their flesh was of a hardness that would satisfy me, so I made them strip naked and lie face down on the block of ice. After about fifteen minutes I made them get up. Those whose flesh resembled the substance of statues left quite a distinct impression of their bodies hollowed out in the ice; the others left only a very vague imprint of flabby flesh incapable of competing with the solidified snow. Both groups of women were led into the second room, but while the first were having their heads and bodies gently shaved so that they no longer retained any animal qualities, not even their hair, the rest I had whipped until they bled, in the knowledge that flagellation is excellent for firming the flesh. Only the first group of women, once they were quite smooth and shiny from head to foot, was admitted into the last room where I made love to them, lying on the marble flagstones which I preferred to any soft cushion or relaxing divan, owing to their hardness and geometrical precision. Almost always I would inflict wounds on them with my teeth or they would get up covered in bruises caused by the spasmodic impact of their bodies on the flagstones. So then I would cover them with jewels which concealed their injuries, while at the same time uplifting my soul with their brilliance and subduing the miserable rancour of the slaves.

Making love thus, to these alabaster women with skulls balder than stones, who were almost as hard and white as the bare floor supporting their limbs, seemed to me like travelling across glaciers, walking for hours through fields of snow scarcely touched by the glowing red sun to which winter lent a clear, metallic aspect. I was no longer caressing women but frozen rivers and icy ponds upon which my thoughts could glide lovingly like a crowd of skaters tracing (imaginary diamonds on this imaginary mirror) the only female name I have ever been able to tolerate, because of its delightful coldness: I mean AURORA… At its climax, however, my pleasure was only ever like an immense thaw, with the ice breaking up into pieces and the sinuous human bodies being reinstated in its dirty waters. Consequently these delights left me completely unsatisfied, and I was forced to look for something else.

Every night I secretly prowled around the vicinity of the temple, but I was no longer content as I had been in the past to wish vaguely that the sky might cave in. Today my hatred craved more substantial nourishment, and so I always carried with me a bottle and a knife. Not a day came without it being discovered at dawn that one of my former friends had been mysteriously murdered and bled like a pig. It would have been easy to discover the murderer, given the surgical precision of the wounds which were obviously the work of a very steady hand practised in the art of sacrifice. Assuming that I was suspected of the crimes, however, it is obvious that no one would have dared breathe a word of it, such was the fear inspired by my high office.

Returning from these nocturnal expeditions, I would give free rein to my frenzied joy, making love to the statues and columns and polluting even the stones on the roads and the tiniest pebbles on the smallest paths. It was thanks to this that I conceived the idea which would allow my metaphysical passion to reach its zenith.

One night, when I had cut the throat of the last of my friends and had myself returned covered in blood with strange phosphorescences lodged in my wounds, I dismissed all the women from my palace. Once it was suitably dried I crushed the vile blood of my victims (carefully collected with the aid of my bottle) and from its fragments I made myself a diadem which I wore night and day all alone in my palace. As for the knife, that metal triangle designed for the most marvellous geometric demonstrations of love and death, I buried it beneath the central flagstone in the marble room, still stained here and there with spots of blood.

Now every night, on this same spot where previously I had slept with women, I would make love alone or more precisely, to the cold stone flag which covered the knife. I gradually sharpened my teeth on the motionless grindstone of the flags, I clasped the floor with my arms open in the shape of a cross, and at these moments I truly possessed the entire world with its retinue of laws and cardinal points, my body thrusting its sensual arches directly over the central point around which the whole universe was concentrically assembled: the gleaming sexual blade which was the very soul of the murderous knife.

In this estimable knife I had just found the only object capable of translating all the diversity of my mind into concrete form, the one figure capable of becoming the sole recipient of my love. In the vague obscurity of its hiding-place the threefold purity of its angles came into play. Cold as a star and polished as if by countless caresses, it could trigger the advent of cruelty at the very moment when it stood erect like a penis, the very image of rigidity. It was the perfect instrument — sharp as wit, hard and keen as the edges of its metal — a unique triangle symbolising the only trinity I deign to recognise:

PURITY, COLDNESS

and

CRUELTY.

However, drunk with all the pride in the world after this discovery, I did not want it to stop there. Grandiloquent ruler that I was, I believed that nothing lay beyond my grasp, and it was this belief which brought about my downfall.

The temple whose rituals of worship had by inheritance been entrusted to my care was dedicated (by a strange quirk of fate!) to *Femininity*. Each part of this temple corresponded to one of the parts of a woman's body. Thus the entrance was through two side doors always wide open which represented her hands. Not far away stood her feet, two plinths supporting tortoiseshell statuettes. Two fine blocks of marble lying side by side symbolised her thighs, and a large vase filled with fruit and flowers was supposed to represent her hips. In the centre of a slightly convex courtyard which was her stomach, her navel lay like a deep, hollow well. Further on, her breasts were visible as two equal hemispheres covered in white leather. Her armpits were two little grottoes entirely carpeted with ivy; her hair, a forest; her buttocks, two tombstones separated by a ravine; her eyes, two little almond-shaped pools each set beneath an archway and constantly full of water and fish; her mouth, an aviary; her nose, a cypress tree round which on feast days people would place rotting meat; her ears, two spiral staircases disappearing into the ground; her neck, a marble column; finally, her sexual organs were represented by a huge shell nestling in furs and concealing a square underground chamber which was her womb.

It was this temple (separated from the sea by a simple wall which was all that prevented the water from engulfing it, so that it was quite clear that everything feminine is barely removed from celestial attractions, nature's revolutions and the changing of the seasons), it was this temple, I say, whose structure I decided to modify in order to make it more in keeping with my divinity. A dreadful sacrilege, perhaps more reprehensible in the eyes of men than all the murders I had previously committed, and of which I was soon to reap the consequences.

I began by having the forest of hair cut down and the furs of her vulva and leather of her breasts replaced by pieces of cloth on to which I had glued tiny particles of rock (this was later to be known as *emery cloth*). In place of the ivy in her armpits I planted pins on which I burned balls of resin on feast days. For the cypress of her nose I substituted a butcher's hook on which the meat would henceforth be hung. Instead of the vase of fruit and flowers which stupidly represented her hips, I put a big glass jar full of set squares and compasses. I unscrupulously caught the fish swimming in her eyes and replaced them with lifeless floats. Similarly I removed the cage filled with birds which symbolised her mouth, and in its place I installed a container full of serpents set between two saws which I declared to be her jaws. On the tip of each breast I planted a spearhead. Above the portal of each hand I hung a spade and a pick. Into the well of her navel I dropped a plumbline, a sort of internal umbilical cord which fell straight to the bottom of the inner surface. I did not tamper with her thighs, feet, ears, neck, buttocks or vagina, but in the cavity of her womb, in place of the secret object (and today more than ever, now that my perdition is certain, nothing can stop me revealing its nature — it was an exact reproduction in miniature of the whole temple, with a womb which itself concealed an even smaller reproduction, and so on *ad infinitum*) I set a mantrap, a few bottle bottoms and the finger of a hanged man, thereby nipping in the bud the endless series of reproductions. On the ceiling of this womb was depicted a starlit night resembling the real night which cast its spell on the temple, and here I went so far as to paint my name, framed by the principal figures of geometry, in black on a white background, which clearly indicated my definite intention of refusing to consider the world as anything other than a function of myself, a slave white with terror beneath the black heel of my thoughts.

I had counted on the fear I inspired and the sacred character conferred on me by my office to stifle any show of resentment among the people, but I was mistaken in my calculations. When the first feast day arrived and the gates of the temple were opened wide allowing the crowd to enter and see the changes I had wrought, whereas I had reckoned on either mere dumb amazement on their part or else transfixed consternation, in fact there arose a long murmur and all kinds of insults streamed forth from every mouth; then, suddenly, I was pelted with a hail of stones. The slopes of my face became etched with bloody zigzags like the jagged paths scratched by lightning on the cheeks of a mountain. Surprised by the swiftness of such an unexpected attack, I was hit by a second volley of projectiles while still paralysed with astonishment. This time my right cheekbone was laid bare, and it protruded like a pebble from the semicircular ditch which ringed my right eye. I faltered for a moment, but recovering my balance almost immediately I ran to the huge shell, making as if to lift it and hurl it at my assailants. The latter dispersed forthwith, not wishing even indirectly to cause the breakage of this sacred object which in their judgement would have been an even more ominous sacrilege against the Deity than all those I might have committed.

For the moment I was safe, but I had not the slightest illusion as to the temporary nature of this salvation. Now that I was considered sacrilegious, in fact, there was no longer anything inviolable about my life; on the contrary, the important thing was not to preserve it but rather to purify the temple by destroying it. Of this I had just had positive proof when a moment ago the people had tried to stone me to death.

Back inside my palace I watched the movements of the crowd through the wire mesh of a window. I saw that after dispersing they had re-formed, not as a solid mass but in an enormous semicircle the ends of which stretched to the sea and in the middle stood the temple and my palace. I realised that they wanted to deprive me of all means of escape in order to have me at their mercy.

Far from feeling the slightest fear at this situation, I had from the start of the adventure felt suddenly imbued with a strange courage, as if my pride at being hated and directly threatened by those I considered the most appalling vermin had delivered me from all mortal anguish, at the same time elevating me at once to the rank of transcendental king, a rank to which I had never ceased to aspire from the moment I was born.

My past cowardice was no longer of any significance. As calm as the sovereign on a chess-board, surrounded by the thousands of intersecting paths of the other pieces, I stayed inside my palace, insensitive to the web of danger which I imagined grew ever larger around me, woven by the invisible hands of those I was now convinced had sworn to kill me. For a second, while I was being attacked, I had thought of letting myself be stoned to death. There was something about the minerality of this death which did indeed attract me, but on the other hand I thought it better all the same, since I was doomed, to try to take a few others with me. Also, despite my utter contempt for whatever traps they might set for me and the plan they had no doubt hatched at very least to starve me to death by cutting me off completely from the outside world (this must have been the reason for the semicircular position they had taken up and which they seemed set to maintain), I resolved not to grant my enemies such an easy victory and at least to deprive them of the pleasure of fighting over my corpse.

In order to carry out my plan (and this was only a few days ago), I began by building myself a crude boat with a few pieces of wood and a large length of canvas found in an attic. I filled it up with all the provisions I could find so as to keep hunger and thirst at bay for as long as possible. I had taken care to carry out this construction close to the sea wall, so that my barque would have no difficulty putting to sea when the time came.

Once my work was finished I went into the marble room I had previously had converted in my palace, lifted up the central flagstone beneath which lay my knife and, seizing this object and placing it between my teeth, I let the stone slab fall silently back into place and returned to hide myself in the barque. From this moment it became my only — and probably my last — dwelling place: I have now been on board for seven days and seven nights and am awaiting the imminent equinox in order to execute my plan.

It is the stones that will avenge me. When the tide is at its most violent, which according to astronomy will occur in two days, I will insert the tip of my knife between the central stones of the sea wall, loosening the keystone, and the waves will flood in and tear down the rest of the wall, engulfing perhaps for ever the temple out of whose walls these despicable men would so much have liked to drive me.

I have written my story on this sheet of metal which in a few moments I will conceal in the deep vault of the sacred womb, knowing full well that there is only a very slim chance of its ever being discovered, but because I nevertheless want to arrange for myself the possibility of a posthumous and reputedly unhealthy pleasure (by thus revealing the naked truth of myself, perhaps, to a future reader) similar to the pleasure I felt when on ritual feast days I would expose myself in that outfit with the scarlet toque and white silk corset with two stiffened pouches which made me look exactly like the male sexual organ.

In a very few hours the sea wall will be breached and I will set sail, as tranquil as a statue, in the flimsy vessel I have built with my own hands, laughing at the disappointment of those who were already imagining that they would be my executioners. Not only will their revered shrine be destroyed, but the slower ones among them who do not flee swiftly enough will certainly perish in the flood, and this fills my heart with the greatest possible joy. While my triangular sail still solves the equation whose two unknowns are the wind and the waves, I will pour out insults on every living thing beneath the skies. I will curse all this shapeless vegetation and seek to poison the sea with my spittle.

As for my knife, sole agent of the blood of several murders and the instigator of this final tumult, I will treasure it because it alone will enable me, when all my supplies are exhausted and my boat lost, doubtless for ever, in the liquid swamp of the waves (for I am not unaware that it would need an extraordinary stroke of fortune for this escape to bring me to a place where I might easily land), to elude death's vile enslavement by putting an end to my own life, in a manner both geometric and majestic, the hilt of the dagger sunk deep into my flesh marking an eternal cross on my heart, a sign more noble than any wretched crucifix, because no man is nailed to it for the sake of pity, and because it therefore remains a pure metallic star, its crystalline branches stretched taut from one side to the other, and not the rotten gallows bearing the bleeding carcass of one who only ever loved two acts fit for washing down the sink: lamentation and self-sacrifice.

In witness whereof I sign my name as a man now assured, thanks to the tip of an implement, of his ability to become immortal:

DAMOCLES SIRIEL."

Having finished deciphering this document, the man who had just been the first to read it dropped the sheet of metal on the ground and remained motionless for a while, his face frozen in a vacant smile suggesting little intelligence. However, after a few minutes of reflection he rose, took off the beige wool sweater covering his torso, picked up the story of Damocles Siriel (the rigid undulations of which left their mark in the sand) and wrapped it in this garment. Then he strode off in the opposite direction to the sea, pitilessly crunching beneath the thick soles of his boots the earth baked hard by the sun.

This young man dressed like an athlete with clean-shaven lips was an Anglo-Saxon writer, the author of two important books: *Jesus Christ, Masochist* and *Mother Country and Aunt Country*, a pornographic novel.

That night the spectre of Aurora flew over the sleeping countryside and no person living or dead — no more Damocles than the man in the white dinner-jacket, the traveller in yellow boots or even myself — could have said whether her presence was real or imaginary, so light was her ghostly apparel, one little swirl of wind lost among so many others!

"Baying dogs who intoxicate the moon with your howls, your gullets, almost as cold as death, are strange caverns where no potion of oblivion is concocted but rather a blackish mixture which oozes drop by drop into the nocturnal wells when the hour of couch-grass and brambles strikes, in the sombre bell tower which in days gone by was filled, at the mere approach of Aurora, with the howling carillon of a desperate baptism. Despite the medley of colours in your coats, stray dogs, and the soft pinkish tinge of your jowls, you will be unable, in the blue shadows where yellow stars float like wisps of straw — the first compasses — to revive except in appearance the faded prestige of colour. The harvest fan is gathered in, the inner pigments have decomposed, the bony architecture is crumbling and although the variously coloured dust particles swirl up to paint the clouds, it is a white pallor which reigns supreme and which extends the foliage of its kingdom over this whole page of the world like that dried-up, colourless tree which always dominates the frontispiece of a prophetic book..."

The sound of mewing, however, slipped between the unbounded grooves of the night, a storm of barking answered it, and the shadow of Aurora vanished into the mist, among the broken clouds which none of these strident noises had managed to disperse.

# IV.

Hundreds of miles from the sea, far from any kind of lake or stream in a region where the dryness stemming directly from the heat of the sun battles only against the multiple yet minuscule rivers of rain which run from the sky each year, there lies a labyrinth of the dead hollowed out in the ground, a sort of cirque or circular creek at the bottom of which arcs of a circle and segments of straight lines are cut into the earth at different depths like the inner casing of a watch. This gigantic chronometer, this maze constructed below ground level but all of whose parts, cog-wheels and cavities, are left open to the sky, is the remote place where corpses are refined, where strange hands lay them out naked on the red clay, deep down in this basin of time, or else beneath subterranean domes built all around in the shape of beehives so that the alchemical egg of air contained within the rough stone walls may transform them into invisible honey.

This opening in the ground, where birds and the heaviest clouds nestle without difficulty, was the grave in which the spectre of Aurora had taken up residence, believing that the sharp cleaver of its lines and curves would bring forth from her imaginary body a honey all the sweeter for being more minutely divided.

The transformation of corpses into spectres and then into honey is not an operation noted for its simplicity. First the corrosive effluvia emitted by the earth must have destroyed all the flesh, and the bones must have combined with the red clay, for only then can the spectre free itself, and from its flimsy wings (mortified between the molecules of air now constituting innumerable little walls) the honey is produced, its nature and quality varying according to the depth and also the shape of the place where this metamorphosis occurs. It is from the finest honey that the magnetic currents are formed which generate lightning, the sudden brilliance of the dead between two clouds grown heavy with prophecies. The coarsest honey is used in the making of heavenly manna, a veritable syrup of death with the sickly smell of patent medicine.

Aurora, for her part, planned to return to earth with the phantasmagoria of magical storms, and for this reason her spectre had concealed itself in the very depths of this strange factory bereft of fly-wheels and drive-belts.

It is futile, however, to remain any longer at the spot where, despite her nightly jaunts, Aurora spins such a fine cocoon, and it would be better to adopt the unctuous speed of a sly flash of lightning and to turn back towards the sea, that vast avenue along which flows the feverish traffic of eternal events and encounters.

At noon precisely on the day after the young man in fawn boots had made his discovery, a ray of sunshine fell directly from its zenith on to a little wisp of foam forming the crest of one of the biggest waves in this ocean furrowed by so many secretly powered ships. The foam evaporated, then rose towards the zenith and merged with a cloud. At that moment the wind blew, violently driving the cloud towards land so that when it turned into rain, the atmospheric conditions having changed, the droplet formed by the original wisp of foam fell on the forehead of the traveller in yellow boots who had fallen asleep in the middle of a vast plain. Startled by this spot of rain signalling the onset of a shower, the traveller awoke and hastily resumed his journey, abandoning the comfortable bed of flattened corn which had become moulded to the shape of his body as he lay in the field, so that only a few hours later when the shower had ceased another traveller crossing the field noticed this wonderful bed and did not hesitate, since it was unoccupied, to lie down there for a rest.

Far from being turned out like a sportsman riddled with snobbery or an intellectual in search of adventure on the road, this second traveller was dressed like an out-and-out vagabond, covered more with grubby patches and darns made with string than with the rough material from which his suit must originally have been cut. Although his face was deeply tanned by the sun and etched with long lines which were no doubt the result of his having suffered all kinds of hardship, he looked extremely young, almost like a child. His long bushy locks scrawled their signature across his forehead and his long thin hands (each one a narrow framework of nerves and bones) rose now and again like curious winged creatures with five beaks to brush away this troublesome hair. A hawk with extremely keen sight would have been able to discern on the little finger of his left hand a very thin band of gold hardly wider than a thread, but round the edges of which were carved rats that seemed to be devouring the substance of the ring. Yet there was no obvious explanation as to how a poor vagabond like this came to be wearing such a ring of gold.

The strange boy lay down, therefore, so as to let the tiredness rising within him like steam wearing out the inside of a boiler escape through every pore of his motionless body. With his eyes half closed he mused on this tiredness which did not seem like something internal, emanating from his body and confined to the limits of that body, but rather an external evil imported from outside by the trees on the roads and the landscapes alongside them, weary of being dragged along in this way by gazes cast like cables so as to make them group together in harmonious panoramas and views. It was not his own tiredness he carried within him but that of all the open country he had crossed and which, wounded by this human arrow piercing it through and through, was trying to stop him by hampering his movements with a thousand ties and coagulating the atmosphere around him so that the air he breathed to make his blood less heavy was thicker than the blood itself. His step was still as brisk as before, but the landscape around him unfolded more slowly. For this reason he could but consider himself the victim of a plot hatched by the natural environment, a conspiracy of trees and streams anxious at all costs to avoid the nauseating instability of "things seen" inflicted on them by the footsteps of the traveller.

The latter now had his eyes completely closed and since nothing more could penetrate his eyelids he found rest at last, as if a sort of peace treaty had been signed for a few hours between nature and himself, until the opening of his eyes and his getting to his feet prior to setting off once more signalled the outbreak of another war, different perhaps owing to the traveller's change of direction on the one hand, and the natural elements joining battle on the other, but no less fascinating than the first... His body, heavy with all the visual sensations he had derived from the world, was at this moment gradually emptying itself, replacing this ballast made up of different materials with the lighter sand found on the boundless shores of the imagination.

When all the memories of the places he had seen during the day had faded from his mind, several shapes emerged which he was quite unable to perceive in their entirety but whose outlines he vaguely sensed, just as one can remember an angle or curve without recalling in the slightest the object to which each belonged, or even ascribing this angle or curve to a completely different object.

First he glimpsed several girls as if through the branches of a hedge. Their fingers worked tirelessly threading necklaces, and every so often some of them would drop a too brightly coloured bead on the ground with a faint cry. He also saw prostitutes encountered in the street or in dreams. On the corner of a narrow lane made all the more gloomy by its proximity to the blazing lights of a late-night restaurant, one evening when he was starving one of these women had given him not bread but a packet of cigarettes decorated with an ace of clubs, and each of these cigarettes had given rise to a mirage. The first had conjured up an entire foreign city and himself wandering its streets. A woman had put her arms round him just as a car approaching from the same direction as herself paralysed him in the glare of its headlights; for a second he had remained transfixed by this twin gaze, while the woman spoke to him in various tongues one of which was unknown to him. The thickest smoke from the last cigarette had formed a fearsome creature whose bestial laughter had tormented him all night long; sumptuous castles of flesh appeared through the trees of its every movement, and behind the window panes of alcohol could be seen trophies brought back from copious hunts…

Sensing, however, that he was in danger of becoming bogged down for ever in the stench of this sentimental swamp, the traveller opened his eyes wide, thereby abruptly closing the gates of fantasy. He then took a piece of stale bread from his haversack and began to eat it, at the same time pulling out of his pocket a little book whose title, embossed on the worn cover, indicated that it was the collected major works of Paracelsus.

On the first page of this volume was a portrait of Paracelsus in profile, next to a water tank in a Roman edifice; his eye was fixed on a nest of branches crowning an isolated column like a capital, and in his right hand he held a mirror in which some clouds were reflected. Towards the middle of the book Paracelsus was shown full-face and bareheaded, dressed in a black doublet with his hands resting on a long sword whose hilt and hand-guard formed an astrolabe. At his throat hung a rich necklace of colourful stones, each of which was engraved with an animal also represented in an identical colour on the planisphere of the astrolabe. On the blade of this astral sword (designed to smite God and his entire creation?) the finest damascening repeated all along the weapon showed the following rebus: a tank full of water, the Greek letter ρ and the Egyptian monkey-god Râh, a rebus which could only read "Eau-Rô-Râh."[7]

Finally, on the last page, like a sort of diagram summarising the content of the text, was a reproduction of the escutcheon of Paracelsus, comprising a red alembic drawn on a star-studded black background inside which burned a white salamander and from which blond hair rose like wisps of smoke. The whole thing was accompanied by this motto, most appropriate for the greatest man ever to seek the Philosophers' Stone:

OR AURA.[8]

This was the book (doubtless picked up in some hovel where he had been shown hospitality for a night) the young vagabond began to read when he no longer wished the octopus of his heart to clasp him in its sentimental tentacles.

## BOOK ONE

*Of the stone, its nature and properties*

When God had extracted the world from the substance of his decrepit body a few eternal minutes before dying (for the universe is but the ashes of a dead god), the Philosophers' Stone let out the first murmurings of its tender vertebrae, an infant's wail like the plaintive cry of the mandrake when it is torn from the soil around the gibbet under whose sign its fibres have formed. This moaning, risen from an unknown cellar where the wine of future acts lay maturing, was the first to resound through the universe in childbirth, and its rocky syllables compose the true human name of the Stone,[9] a name which several people know and sometimes speak, though not one of them knows to which miraculous object this name really applies. This stone, born of the earth which was bitten to its red core by the first ray of the sun, corresponds so perfectly to the word which denotes it that it would suffice merely to analyse each of its syllables and letters for it to be revealed in all the glory of its true nature and the dazzling brilliance of its properties. However, such an analysis is impossible for most men because they would have to trace the variations on the name of the Stone right to the very last ramifications of their sounds, a work of which no man has as yet shown himself capable, owing to his lack of the rigid yet at the same time many-faceted mind needed to solve this problem.

Thus the Philosophers' Stone was born at the same time as the world, but unlike the latter it is not subject to the yoke of space and time, a heavy beam fit only for that great, sullen, slow-moving ox which is the universe with its stinking entrails full of the cud of sadness, and not for the Stone, this weightless receptacle of infinite metamorphoses, when the friable knuckle-bones of life and death knock together almost to cracking-point in the palm of destiny.

A strange colour suffuses it; it is white, but a white born of the union of all colours and not the pale tint whose reflection plays ominously on the surface of the corpuscles of nothingness, absolutely indivisible and therefore resembling zero. It is this white, the white of ghosts and nights without sleep, richer than any colour, which distinguishes the Stone from all other substances, but it is also this white, thanks to its apparent neutrality, which renders it elusive and multiform, vanishing more swiftly than a drop of water through the side of a porous jug or a spark flying close to the crater of a volcano.

Men say that there are four paths which may lead to the Stone: the path of flames, the path of winds, the path of seas and the path of roads (fire, air, water and earth), but none of these paths is the right one, for in order to reach it a single path is needed in which the four elements are united and merged into one. This is because of the very texture of the Stone and the external properties with which it is endowed.

This stone is brittle and capable of crystallising in various ways like deceit, but at its centre it bears the tiniest fragment of a needle, a pointed speck which provides it with an internal armour of truth. Heat it up and it will float in the air like a fairy. Cool it down and it will become hard like a warrior of the Mycenaean age when men still used rocks for breastplates. At normal temperature it is neither solid nor fluid, neither male nor female, yet somehow feminine nevertheless, owing to its unconquerable variance and unchanging transparency which make of it an atmosphere, the suggestion of an idea rather than a clearly defined syllogism.

Its avatars are numberless. It was present at every miracle recorded in the history of mankind, hidden sometimes in a horse's hoof, sometimes in the clouded brow of a miracle-worker or else in the blinding spittle of the unbeliever. It burned in every furnace, whirled between every moving stratification of the wind, flowed with every spring and played a part in the gradual germination of the grain in every field. Yet it remains unique and eternally true to itself, forever locked in the imaginary figure which the mind one day saw fit to invent. The secret of the Eleusinian Mysteries is nothing other than the means by which to discover this form. The same is true of the symbol of Pythia at Delphi whose name derives from the root common to these two words: *putrescere* and *putare*. The pyramids of Egypt conceal nothing else in the geometric arcana of their structures and finally the alchemical research of my predecessors has no other aim than to trace the fictitious outline of this imagined reality — the guarantee of eternal power.

This Stone is a funeral urn which controls the process of putrefaction, but it too is capable of putrefying when it changes into a living creature and consequently becomes subject to putrescence. At once the cause of putrefaction and itself putrefied, it is the very essence of purity, owing to its perpetual undulation which is represented by hair, its dominant symbol. Purifying and purified, it is the sign of thought.

I am forced to disguise the truth with this crude apologue, but I must say that in reality, where this Stone is concerned, there can be no question of putrefaction, purity or thought. None of these terms has any meaning relative to the Stone as it stands in the absolute, since they are caught on the treadmill of time from which it is liberated, and even the word "relative" which I use in conjunction with its name is almost a breach of logic when applied to this Stone. At most I could speak of its transformations, the multiple guises it can assume and also perhaps the hidden flaw which allows man to possess it, thus proving it vulnerable — a veritable Achilles' heel, a misfortune it owes to the fact that it is a thing created, albeit by a dead god, but *created* nevertheless.

There is no need for me to elaborate on the metamorphoses undergone by this Stone. At every turn of world history its traces may be seen without the need for any great perspicacity, and every treatise on the human arts, from agricultural work to the works of the intellect, bears its mark, clearly visible to any eye which is not either short-sighted or blinded by prejudice. On the other hand I might usefully say a few words about its weak point, the chink in its armour which means that to seek it denotes merely a hint of temerity rather than sheer madness.

This fault in construction, inherent in its created condition, is its personality, which means that to a certain extent it is endowed with feelings. That first cry emitted by its vertebrae as it emerged from the chaos of crude gases is a sure sign of this weakness. It goes through its metamorphoses as if through a rolling-mill where pain is sharpened. It is not of course sensitive in the same way as humans, and it remains far above laughter and tears (though it can sometimes take on their appearance), but its stony cells understand the word TORTURE and the secret anguish which slowly emerges from every stone. This is the one thread attaching it to the world, without which it would be as imperceptible as a void, but this thread also denies it full status as the absolute, though its possession allows us to sound the depths of the absolute, to cast nets which will one day perhaps bring in a rich haul of treasure.

So now the time has come to state the main property of this Stone: though it still retains some link with the universe it belongs to the absolute, or perhaps more precisely it has its niche in the wall of the absolute, like the recess hollowed out for an idol. It is thanks to this unique notch that if we succeed in gaining mastery over the Stone, which in this case will serve us as a finger-nail, it will be possible to get some sort of hold on the otherwise completely smooth wall of the absolute. Then, using all our strength to grip this tiny indentation, we will cling to the wall so that through this contact it transmits to us some of its power, thereby making absolutes of us too, veritable microcosms who contain in miniature all the properties of the universe captured in their totality and who are consequently capable of governing the universe in our turn. Thus the circle of our metaphysical destiny will have been squared and its motion perpetuated.

For many years I have devoted my life to this highly ambitious project. I am well aware of the hazardous, indeed by definition impossible nature of such an enterprise, the success of which would amount to dominion over the absolute, that is to say the establishment of a relation between it and myself, which is quite obviously a contradiction. Yet I have confidence in the Stone and am certain that if I manage to discover it, its marvellous powers will not disappoint me. Moreover, various adventures whose stories I have read tend to give me hope. It is appropriate to cite them here — not without a certain irony perhaps — although I am convinced that these stories are intimately related to the search for the Stone, despite the fact that this relationship would seem to be well-hidden:

## STORY OF THE PRESCIENT PRISONER

Towards the end of the twelfth century, in a town in the north of Italy, there was a poor man, a potter by trade, who was incarcerated because his work did not bring in enough money to pay the debts he had incurred trying to establish his business. For several years he remained shut away in isolation at the very top of a castle keep. Deprived of all other recreation, he spent his days drawing graphs, whose meaning none of his gaolers understood, on a slate which they had agreed to let him use. One day the prison fell down. Among the other corpses they found the body of the potter still clasping the slate tightly to his chest. On this slate were drawn the exact lines of the cracks which had caused the walls of the prison to crumble, though these had been invisible until the very moment of the accident.

## STORY OF THE CLOCK-WOMAN

In a trading city belonging to the Hanseatic League, the town-hall clock was adorned with an automaton in the form of a woman with phosphorescent veins who, when the hour struck, would move round the clock once for every chime escorted by three knights. Noticing a girl who was strangely similar to the woman of the clock at a window of the town hall, a young man who had only been in the city a short time slipped into the building one night. The next morning passers-by found him dead in front of the town hall, beside the clock-woman who had fallen from her plinth and broken into pieces, without there being the slightest indication as to how this tragedy could have occurred.

## STORY OF THE METEOR KING

In a small Central-European principality, a most cruel tyrant was held in contempt by his entire people. A young girl decided to rid her country of this man. Waiting until it was mid-summer — the season when meteorites most frequently fall to Earth — she walked through the countryside one night until she managed to find one of these mineral objects. Having moistened it with a few drops of her menstrual blood, she stole into the tyrant's chamber and placed the celestial stone she had thus prepared between two fleurons of his crown. When the moon changed and the tyrant, as was his wont, returned to his palace after a night of dissolute debauchery, he was suddenly lifted up into the air by his crown and in a few moments had vanished like a flaming torch in the direction of Orion's nebula.

### STORY DEDICATED TO THE RECKLESS

Deep in an Alpine valley, a man let it be commonly known that he wished to die struck by lightning. Whenever possible he chose to go out on stormy days, climbing the highest and therefore most exposed peaks. One morning, after the thunder had raged all night, his body was found close to a peak, apparently struck by lightning. A visiting surgeon who examined the corpse, however, noted that he had died of fright, his heart having burst.

These four tales could, if need be, provide whoever knew how to interpret them with the basic principles of conduct leading to the discovery of the Stone. I myself could expound these rules at great length. However, after this apparently humorous digression, it is time I returned to the subject which I set out to discuss in this chapter.

This Stone is not only a body subject to metamorphosis and capable of triggering metamorphoses in other bodies; it is as metamorphosis itself, the very entity of motion. If its only possible medium is said by alchemists to be the substance they call *philosophers' mercury*, then it is because this fluid alone moves quickly enough to follow it into its many and varied recesses. It must not be forgotten, moreover, that the Stone is linked to the revolutions of the stars and that every moving object has an effect upon it. Not a single pebble falls, hurled by a pilferer into the branches of a tree heavy with fruit, not a single arrow lodges in its wooden target, shot by means of the sudden release of a bow string, and not a single wisp of smoke rises from the brick chimney of the laboratory of an alchemist searching for this very Stone, without their having some impact upon it. It connives with all movement, and this complicity ranges from the migration of birds and the journeys of the planets which regulate the tides, to the different mental processes undergone by those who seek the Stone and the molecular transformations of the substances they heat up in their damaged retorts.

Here, however, I should say that in my opinion it is a mistake to use alchemical methods to further this research. Astrology might well give better results. All the same, I believe that we should think of our bodies not simply as scaled-down versions of the heavens but also as actual stills and that, conversely, this Stone is in a way human. given that it has feelings. Above all we must therefore observe the human body, and it is to this study that I have primarily devoted myself.

For a long time now I have channelled my research in this direction. I observe with passion these caves of the human body in which countless monsters lie hidden. Which watchman lit these fires at the top of this tall hillock of vertebrae? A herd of tactile sensations grazes in the boundless pasture of the skin. This evening the cattle will go to sleep amid the dung in their stable, lying next to the goats of smell, the pigs of taste, the bulls of hearing and the horses of sight. Later, shrouded in a hood of mindless exhaustion, every one of these beasts will of its own accord surrender to the butcher. One strange animal alone, perhaps, will refuse to follow the herd. It is a curious little heap of membranes, white like marble and almost as formless as a jellyfish. It communicates with the stars by means of several holes pierced in its body, but it attracts serpents by its terrible coldness, often more extreme than that of ice.

The human body is also an enormous city with its working-class areas, covered markets and palaces. At night, beneath the windows of merry-making members of the bourgeoisie, prostitutes tout for business along the dark passageways. From time to time a hideous police force carries out raids and after this the corridors of veins turn into the corridors of a prison. The cries of those being tortured, their corpses soon to be thrown to rot naked in the graveyards, rise up to the air holes of the nostrils. Yet perhaps one day the bandits who keep watch in the cave of the heart will mount a surprise attack...

Thus examining the body and likening it in turn to a field given over to grazing animals, to a town populated with whores, policemen and rogues, to (who knows?) a mountain with its glaciers and forests, to a sea with its unknown fish, its seaweed and ships, to a village built in the snow by sealers, to the wooden shack of a gold-miner, to a salt-mine, to a peat-bog full of molluscs and will-o'-the-wisps — having compared the body to all these things in succession, I have come to the conclusion that only the discovery of the Stone could liberate it by substituting freedom for the fate which humiliates it, and that on the other hand the search for the Stone should not be left to the alchemist. I will add that the body is a vast theatre and that there are many possible positions from the top to the bottom of its tiers. I have summarised all this in the following diagram: a still whose steam is hair and in the centre of which burns the *White Salamander*.

This Stone which governs all movement is naturally capable, by virtue of its dominion, of transmuting everything. It can change lead into gold, an old man into a youth, a marsh into firm ground and a courtesan into a fairy. Yet it is essentially unstable and possibly the few who have found it have allowed it to escape before they had time to exploit it. It is therefore of vital importance, should you discover it, to be sure to maintain it in its exact form. The only way to do this is to bind it to yourself within the limits of your arteries and to colour it with your blood, for thus you will restore it to the colour of the red clay which was the first vessel of its formation.

Finally, being metamorphosis and movement, this Stone which gives majesty to Man is of necessity also destruction. More than the ordinary corrosive salt which usurps the name on the pitiful pretext that it eats into the skin, it deserves to be called *infernal stone*,[10] for strictly speaking it is a counter-host since by its intervention Man is made God and not God made Man. Furthermore, that which the derisory celestial remedies claim to effect from on high to below, in other words following the direction of those who bow their heads, it, the Stone, the Philosophers' Stone, accomplishes from below to on high, by the path of pride.

It is with the word *ORGUEIL* (PRIDE) that I shall conclude this first book, pointing out that it is this word which denotes the way in which the transcendental Stone must act, for its first syllable is the word *OR* (GOLD)...

*Out of your rags Eye of death!* [11]

END OF BOOK ONE

Since night was now beginning to fall, the vagabond had to stop reading. He put the book carefully back in his pocket, made himself as comfortable as possible on the bed of corn and only a few minutes later fell asleep.

At dawn he resumed his journey, singing this refrain which he had made up himself:

The honey walls of your feasts
Ha ha Sisters will be inlaid with niello
this rhomboid if the vine bunch
rakes up the spirits beneath your brows

Ha ha the eggs marrow of the Pope
will be soft-boiled Sisters like your calves
this *rond de jambe* if they catch
the anvil of your blacksmiths' eyes

Ha ha of your blacksmiths' eyes.[12]

Around the analytical cemetery where Aurora was to be transformed into a meteor by the agency of the bare earth, four lions lay stretched out, abandoning their vampiric manes to the four winds, and their tails, extending between the mountain ranges, merged with the dried-up streams whose stony skeletons traced their eternally motionless spines through the deep valleys. The eighty claws riveting these beasts to the ground pierced the soil to a remarkable depth, a depth at which it ceases to function as a mole whose soft, brownish eyelids allow no light to filter through, and becomes spangled with indistinct reflections cast by a slumbering lamelliform object similar to mica. Here the layers of earth are arranged in uneven folds just like the creases furrowing a white toga, and the dividing surfaces are like so many superimposed coats covering the geological corpses of several generations of dead tribunes. Between these funerary pillow-slips, almost as straight as the Plimsoll line which bisects the height of a ship, ancient pieces of leather or laurel are sometimes found, but they are made of a shiny black substance which no longer has anything in common with either leather or laurel. This substance is the salt of the earth as it is found in its natural state uncontaminated by living vegetation.

The four wild beasts lay above these sediments of innumerable shrouds, and whenever their roars erupted, spewing lava and resonant scoria, they ravaged the nearest farmland and dwellings beyond the desolate area surrounding the mournful grave over which the lions kept watch. Four coats, each of a different colour and material, covered the internal structure of these animals.

The first was a whitish gas like those nebulous formations seen in the sky when the night is sufficiently clear to enable one to glimpse enough of the stars hidden beneath it. The second spread a sheet of streaked water over the entire space it occupied, like a dark torrent punctuated with abundant white commas of foam, or else the quincuncial net which the retiarius throws over his adversary. The third consisted of a dark-coloured drapery like the dust sheet placed over a piano or a harp which one does not intend to use for a long time. The fourth was a black void like the entrance to an obscene cave or the window framed with wrought iron which looks out on to nothingness.

After the young man in fawn boots, Damocles Siriel, the vagabond with his ring of carved rats and Paracelsus, you may well be wondering, readers, what these four lions lying round her ghost have to do with the story of Aurora, she who when the first clouds of the events I am relating began to knock against each other was just a very pretty woman who lived in the skyscraper of pessimism and was in love with the man in the white dinner-jacket? Put your minds at rest! All these seemingly disparate phenomena are in fact closely related, as indeed any phenomenon is related to any other, be it the bottles of whisky which the man in the white dinner-jacket and I liked to drink in the Tropics, the ace of clubs decorating the packet of cigarettes given to the vagabond by a prostitute or even the coat of arms of Paracelsus, no more meaningful than any of these other things. In order to present a concrete argument to support this thesis, moreover, I shall now proceed to demonstrate how these four lions in fact relate directly to myself.

First I might say that despite their different coats these four lions are equal, and that this word "equal" is equivalent to the Latin pronoun EGO,[13] which means *myself*. Equally I could argue that they possess the same supreme nobility which sculptured the air at the moment of my departure, that great solemn curtain that always substitutes its opaque gravity for the transparency of the wind whenever this slow, profound separation occurs — a rift such as might bring down walls — between the quay on the one hand, which remains a prisoner of its cobblestones and chains, and the vessel on the other, carried away on the tide of the future with its cargo of passengers, provisions, machinery and coffins. I might also point out that the French forename *Léon* comes from the Latin *leo*, meaning lion, but my name is not Léon. So rather than dwell on such comparisons, all somewhat spurious, I will say right away that these four animals were like me because in place of a heart each bore the picture of a two-headed king from a playing card.

Like Damocles Siriel who depicts himself as a transcendental monarch, a wooden figure who reigns over an entire chess-board, I too am a king, but my face is double and printed on paper. The upper face, which is the right way up and which all of you see, is that of an old man with a handsome beard, but it is not what you think. It is merely a jumble of lines which quite by chance happen to have formed a human shape, merely a mass of magnetic points, filings which that magnet you know so well, horseshoe-Intelligence (for that old piece of scrap iron you so carefully picked up at the bend in a path full of potholes, thinking it would bring you luck, is none other than this), has grouped into ears, cheeks, a mouth and a nose… It is only the lower face, however, which constitutes my true portrait, because it is upside down and hanging by the feet. Thus am I eternally suspended from the ghastly gibbet of the universe, and my hair hangs lower than my face as if it wanted to take root, becoming plant-like pillars to help support this over-congested head. The stars are veritable nightmares, phantoms which at night haul in the rope binding my feet. What can I do, my head heavy with this black wine which ebbs from my ankles and builds up inside my ears? What can I do, a grotesque hanged man, when I am weary of sticking my swollen tongue out at the ground, pulling a face which does nothing to alleviate my dizziness? You alone have this foreknowledge, O lions, though the double valve of your hearts does not torture you as this duplicity does me…! This is why I evoke you here, more silent and timeless than the spectre you guard, watchmen that you are, and the ramparts of her charnel-house!

In spite of their coats which were not at all leonine, these four lions were therefore the only possible repositories for my image, as carnivores and consequently my allies when with all the strength of my jaws I call down curses upon men and the world, hoping that the overwhelming harrow of cataclysms will crush them in its teeth and annihilate them.

The first lion was the anathema I cast upon those who gave me birth. That is why it was connected with the clouds, the stars and in short with all those bodies which since time immemorial have presided over births and are the harbingers of destiny. The second, in the form of an eddy and a net, was the world pitted with its weapons and shady resources against me, a gladiator pitched into this unequal battle by the Emperor-God dressed in a toga smeared with sperm, fresh grape juice and excrement, a sinister mercenary come to power at the wish of mere slaves and who, constantly surrounded by his fools, minions and trollops, is not content with putting me to death but also demands of me that I die gracefully. The third, draped in a simple piano cover, was another representation of the world, but the world considered as a musical instrument which henceforth I refuse to play. Let all the virtuosi, their hair greasy with ignorance and curly with vanity, persist in making this keyboard of events vibrate beneath their mechanical fingers, I for my part no longer wish to sound its derisory moral chords which make my fellow men with the hearts of powdered old ladies swoon with ecstasy. The fourth, resembling a void, was obviously the figure of nothingness; it was in the heart of this one that my portrait was, as they say, the "living image" of me. It displayed its double head with pride, the feet of the lower half emerging from the brain of the upper half and *vice versa*. As for the organism enclosing it in its muscular labyrinth, this was in no way different from that of the other three lions, except perhaps for its greater limpidity and its absence of visible entrails and all digestive organs.

It was from deep within this quadruple hiding-place whose walls were even thinner than those of physiological starvation, but sufficiently opaque nevertheless for nothing beyond my image to be visible, that I had attended — present in effigy — the metamorphoses of Aurora, ever since she had lain dead in the grave, beautiful like a lion-tamer armed with the eternal whip of her name, a magical rod following her to the tomb.

The ghost of Aurora had thus lain down on the barren ground of this narrow basin, and various external modifications had already transformed her appearance. At her delicate neck, barely supporting her head crowned with hair which was no longer tawny as before but silver like that of all spectral brides, a necklace of pale beads had appeared. These were pearls formed from her fragile bones made iridescent by the lunar whiteness of her vanished flesh, and this rosary shimmered faintly — Orient of milk and melancholy — like a long line of birds whose journeys from season to season have given their feathers a shiny, slightly pink hue, or the innocent tufts of wool which get caught along prison walls when a flock of sheep has passed that way towards dawn, driven by a shepherd who knows that the whole of the Orient can be contained in a single drop of blood, but that wearing away their fleece on the corners of prison cells does sheep no harm.

When this necklace of mortal concretions was fully formed, a silver lamé dress trimmed with white egret feathers gradually appeared, adorning Aurora's imponderable body, and then a little wire construction rested close to her mouth like the patch of black taffeta worn as a beauty spot in the Regency period, the rigidity of this structure contrasting with the curved line of her lips. I recognised this small metal framework immediately as the tiny edifice, reduced to a mere skeleton, which I am in the habit of placing on any object whose softness I wish to gauge.

Thus Aurora lay stretched out, her eyes closed and her arms close to her body, and I watched this thread-like construction marking the unworldly screen of her cheek with delicate, well-defined shadows which brought out its freshness, irreducible even to this subtle geometry. The four lions in whose hearts I was symbolically represented seemed to pay not the slightest attention to these events, doubtless of secondary importance as far as they were concerned and bearing no relation to the task to which they were assigned.

When both pearl necklace and wire apparatus had sufficiently activated the springs of their hidden reality they vanished, and the spectre of Aurora was left as before, lying white and transparent on her bed of clay. Only then did the real metamorphosis begin, for these two events had been but a prelude and a laying-down of conditions, as it were. The four lions roared in unison, dug their claws deeper into the ground, and the panoramic transmutation took place.

First of all the echo of the roars woke all the insects in the neighbourhood, who hastened to the spot and in only a few minutes had devoured all the clay in the grave where the shade of Aurora lay, so that she was soon left suspended in the air without any kind of support. Next a long serpent made of pieces of wood — like those toys it is customary to give children in certain countries of the Far East — emerged from Aurora's mouth and arranged its coils in the shape of a figure **3**. On the site of the grave there now rose up a hive filled with bees, and these tumultuous insects added their humming to the roaring of the lions, while the reptilian **3** wound its lower coil around Aurora's waist, at the same time using its upper angle to hook itself on to the point marking the intersection of the four beasts' quadruple gaze and the imaginary line joining the top of the beehive to the pole-star.

Behind the figure 3 and isolated from any supporting structure there rose a tall window with a finely worked iron balcony consisting of interlaced figures and letters. In front of this rectangle of vitreous material, Aurora swung on the end of the serpentine belt girding her loins. Suddenly, however, a light shone behind the slightly misted panes of glass and a hand, flinging open the two casements of the window, came to rest on the rail of the balcony. The figure 3 was immediately split in half, giving rise to two objects, the upper, horizontal bar with its bevelled end changing into a whip and the whole of the lower part (in which Aurora's body was caught) becoming a sickle which remained suspended between earth and sky, in front of the now dark window whose iron ornamentation, growing like some monstrous plant, had invaded and devoured the entire beehive which from this moment on (always supposing it still contained bees) would have been capable of producing nothing but a honey of figures.

The window catch was a man bound hand and foot, with a wax face and an artificial right arm. When Aurora's body, resting on the blade of the sickle, had finally been cut in half like the most insignificant of sheaves, the window was swallowed up and the man, freed from his bonds, seized the whip and cracked it several times. Having thus tried out his instrument he approached the lower part of Aurora's body (her stomach and legs, like a statue from which the head and chest had been removed to create the antithesis of a bust) and with great lashes of his whip he sent it into a spinning movement like that which drives a top. Her genital area being constricted by the speed and violence of the lashes which caused her to turn, this fragment of Aurora soon took on the shape of an hour-glass into which the other fragment sank when the sting of a surviving bee made it crumble to dust.

When all the sand had collected in the lower half of the hour-glass (which took twenty-four hours), it condensed to form a small shiny sphere the size of a pea, while the hour-glass itself, losing its glassy transparency and the softness of its curves, changed into an angular solid of black matter, composed of two regular, vertically opposite tetrahedrons. The small shiny sphere, external to this new figure, moved at random in the vicinity of this opacity. It was then that the four lions each let out three roars in turn (so that these roars succeeded one another with approximately the same regularity as the months of the year), thereby causing 12 theatrical trapdoors to open up in the surrounding air, each of which admitted one of the edges of the double tetrahedron shattered by this noise like the walls of a fortified town caused to collapse by the sound of trumpets.

Out of the first trapdoor sprang the month of January, a doddering old grandpa with hands full of sweets and greetings; his worn fur cloak was moth-eaten and his slavering smile was melting, a snow of absurd sayings. The month of February and the month of March leapt up from two adjoining doors, both very elegantly dressed with the faces of shady financiers in whose hands dirty money builds up only to dissolve into showers. April and May came up humming a German song about little girls sadder than the plains of sand when the still-born birds preen their feathers each of which is one of the softer aspects of understanding. Then it was June, letting off its sparkling rocket high in the air, and July with its horrible inanimate walls of sunshine along which no tentacles of ivy creep, barer than the inside of a scorching oven when the bread, which in any case had never been anything but the pitiful potential for future excrement, burns to a cinder and is soon but a blackish dust fit only for painting the faces of the dead. August flashed by, dragging its glorious holidays in the wake of its yacht, the foam of idleness resolving into white droplets, each one nothing but a wasted moment, but more precious by reason of this very waste than any tool which attempts vainly to orchestrate the abject, utilitarian symphony of time on the theme of the clock. September came, that gaoler of carcasses rattling his chains and keys like the spectre of work in the long corridors, the dark, stifling labyrinth which constricts the mind between its damp walls, killing it more effectively than any snake. October and November went colourlessly past, faces eaten away by the light-coloured mud found near lime kilns at the hour when the corpses we believe to be at peace, even as they haunt us, are forced to engage in secret work as desperately hopeless as that which they carried out in their lifetime, work like that of ferns in a coalfield which slowly change without it being possible for even the tiniest green frond to escape from the hideous wheel of colours which turns inexorably round and round from white to black and black to white through yellow, blue, green, purple, brown, grey and red, like a train running ceaselessly in a circle through desolate suburbs, its passengers unable to escape from this eternal moving prison, for even if they could throw themselves under its wheels in order to be crushed to death, the shreds of their flesh would remain stuck fast. After these unfailing distress signals, however, December appeared in the guise of a huge frozen lake, uniformly white beneath the black semicircle of a sky studded with dull dots. The lions roared once more, but their voices were those of hoarse old phonographs and their translucent outlines vanished into the past along with my double face which was already receding into the penumbra of idiotic symbols, that vague limbo inhabited by silly creatures more stupid than stones, with their tin-plate jewellery and clothes cut with a sword from vile ticking. The little shiny ball remained the only mobile particle of this empty, frozen universe and its circular motion, constantly accelerating, rent the air with a shrill cry.

When this cry, every second more high-pitched, had become a final, frenzied screeching, the black vault shattered and the metal sphere broke its orbit then fell, a wingless bird of prey plummeting in a rectilinear dive, into the very centre of the icy surface where a long zigzag fissure appeared whose black lightning spread with an ominous crack, soon stretching as far as the geometric frontier of the horizon. Then Aurora, finer than a meteor, Aurora, revived in the form of this mathematical line, rose up suddenly as lightning, hard and majestic, and clearing with one leap of her electric legs the highest peak crowning the human massif of reason, she went with a shiver to nestle in a cloud which all at once turned blood red, like the marvellous iron blade which will unleash the most terrible tortures.

# V.

Sitting on a milestone against the grassy bank bordering a road which led to the mountains, the vagabond was examining the soles of his shoes, calculating the number of countries he had crossed by the extent to which they were worn away. Hardly had I faded from sight, along with my retinue of four wild beasts who were the vehicle of my image and had witnessed the multiple avatars of Aurora, when he muttered the number "39," which indicated how many towns had surrendered their stony bodies to his strides. Far from these malodorous tracks a cloud moving eastwards carried away the storm which had threatened, and the vagabond could see the reflection of a perfectly clear sky shining in the bumpy hobnails of his shoes. The rotten dough of days, more decayed than any culinary concoction prepared by an impostor, made the camera lucida of time stink as usual, but nothing of this disaster penetrated the sensory world and without fear of putrid fumes the young tramp could fill his lungs with air, invisible metal shot which his blood would attach to the hooves of a thousand swift horses whose curved iron shoes attracted it like intangible magnets.

As always, snatches of sentimental ballads dragged themselves like cripples around his head and many a refrain interrupted its flow between his lips, little waves arriving inexplicably from foreign shores. The frayed fibres of a dried-out rag hanging from the shutters of a distant tumbledown cottage fluttered in the wind, and a lie swept through each of its holes like a tornado with a feeble, velvety moan intended to mask the constant danger, like the sound of a finger-nail on satin brocade whose sole purpose is to conceal the desire to rip it in half. A lament dragged its old blood-stained stumps down a remote pathway in the depths of the vagabond's suburban soul, and he drove this old beggar-woman out with a kick, inciting her certainly not to work but rather to kill or steal. Not a single window opened, no orifice of pity through which would pass the gifts to placate this filthy old woman, and the vagabond remained as inflexible as a mayor, identical for once with every other virtuous person. Meanwhile, the wretched woman began to wail pitifully and her blurred eyes wept shafts of ash. This weak music made the walls grow thinner and all the household noises escaped from their rooms and tumbled on to the street with the soft thud of dung being heaped up when the pitchforks work ever faster, accelerating as the day comes to a close. When midnight struck all that was left of the old woman were tatters of taffeta, and the houses were frozen in silence, gagged by their closed windows. The wailing, however, had not vanished completely as had the town which was its setting, and the vagabond could still hear a few verses buzzing in his head long after pathways and walls had faded like the solar constructions of dust made visible by a single ray of sunshine but erased just as quickly by a single cloud. The vagabond was absent-mindedly twisting his gold ring round his little finger, and just as each carved rat passed over the ridge marking the middle of his finger-bone there was a vocal outburst corresponding to one of the few remaining white points of the blackened, worm-eaten skeleton of his refrain. These disparate notes could be joined together by an imaginary piece of string, and it was this dirty old scrap of rope, not fit even to hang oneself with, which in the end was all that was left within the framework of his head, hanging on the upper beam of ebony wood which ran horizontally above the void spanned by this single plait of hemp, the least worn fibres of which supported their own weight with difficulty, even though this was as negligible as the weight of forsaken scruples.

"Spleen,
satiety,
jinx,
failure,

inadequacy,
misfortune,
adversity,
despair,
distress,
cowardice,
tedium,
fear,
unhappiness,
terror,
disgust,
pain,
suffering,
sorrow,
fate,
fury,
melancholy,
impotence,
rage,
torture,
anxiety,
anguish,
misery,
torment,
uncertainty,
doubt,
disappointment,
disillusion,
disenchantment,
heartbreak,

worry,
sickness,
nightmare,
insomnia,
obliteration,
death,
drought,
annihilation,
slavery,
weariness,
despondency,
rancour,
tiredness,
exhaustion,
shame,
dread,
horror,
fright,
bad luck,
sterility,
nausea,
weakness,
anger,
frenzy,
disturbance,
defeat,
abdication,
ruin,
shipwreck,
catastrophe,

bankruptcy,
perdition,
downfall,
degeneration," murmured the vagabond, letting the yellow rope vibrate in the hollow of his head, "so many words whose gravity I will stubbornly deny, attaching with my own hands to every item in the great shop of rumours a white label with black letters spelling the words NULL AND VOID. Of the myriad torches which once burned in my head I have kept but one wisp, a curl of hair which like a fuse is capable of blowing up all the structures of the day and instituting disorder, a hard bed whose white, crumpled sheets — rivers of rapture — are none the less the only ones which satisfy my heart's desire. When the bolt slips into the lock and fruit falls from the tree, I envy the grey grub which eats its way inside with jaws which although carnivorous are so well designed to savour the freshness. It hollows out a delicate path for itself through the light-coloured density of the flesh, and when the discordant bells of reality chime in with the endless bellowing from the court of stupidity it cracks open the fruit, turning it into a metaphysical bomb deadlier than any device, for it is at the same time as real as a fortune and as unreal as the love of a man who one day murders his bank manager in order to provide for the luxurious needs of a dancer whose stunning poses are like so many branches which she affects in order that our tender glances may rest on them like passing birds. One evening, from the gallery of a music-hall which no one would have dared take upon himself to stop me entering, the look in my eye nullifying the holes in my clothes, I saw a woman with very white skin whose voluptuous body was swinging in mid-air wearing only a bra and G-string made of diamonds. Her trapeze was exactly like the wooden crossbar from which the rope — all that currently occupies my brain — is suspended, but each of her finger-nails and toe-nails gleamed like a tear or a dagger. On the scarlet sea of her lips ships decked with flags sailed by, visible only to me and commanded by my fever, while in the centre of her belly a winding staircase sank from view, an immutable stone vortex leading to a vast substratum softly paved with algae and underwater aureolae. After the curtains had closed, interrupting my view of the stage, the music-hall disappeared and I found myself standing near a waste land strewn

with rotten, rat-infested planks where poisonous flies buzzed and foul phosphorescent larvae tried to climb up my legs. Yet this lock of hair which I have since twisted into a rope had remained stuck to the top of a palisade and I watched it stir in the desperately pulsating wind, the south wind, the whistling wind, the living wind, the dying wind…"

The evocation of this light flotsam — a little silky yellow plant attached to the top of a rough plank and like a will-o'-the-wisp overhanging this deserted suburb of disaster (a term which, although he had denied it, returned again and again with the persistence of a ghost trying to force every door) — had driven any idea of even momentary rest from the vagabond's mind, and he was already getting to his feet, picking up the gnarled stick which helped him negotiate the more difficult paths and setting off again, his hand moving swiftly to check that the only volume he possessed containing the hermetic works of Paracelsus was still tucked inside the pocket of his dirty jacket, between a piece of candle and a crust of bread.

After he had been walking for a few hours and his heels had patterned the soft dust of the road with an entire procession of more or less solemn prints, his customary carefree manner returned and he was only concerned with looking at the trees lined up along the edge of the path like a double row of lighted candles planted along a sumptuously laid table in the home of people who insist on celebrating properly the birthday of a very small child, as yet completely unaware of time's stratagems. Like those wax columns, each tree he passed represented a day gone by, and looking straight ahead the vagabond could have calculated how many days he still had left to live, simply by counting the number of trees separating him from the horizon which was brought closer and rendered uneven by the snowy mass of a very high mountain. This mountain, however, was a far more attractive sight than the monotonous, almost straight avenue which led to it, and with newly fired curiosity the vagabond observed the cluster of events unfolding halfway up the main peak, to the tip of which were fastened various ropes tautened at different angles whose diverging lines were diminished by the distance so that in spite of their size they appeared even thinner than the hairs whose loose, blond fibres had formed the wonderful tuft in the mind of the tramp.

"When mountaineers, generally spurred on by the most wretched vanity, set off at daybreak to attempt the ascent of an extremely steep peak, they divest themselves of all superfluous objects so as to make themselves as light as possible, but they almost always forget to leave behind their abstract baggage of prejudice in the hollow of this plain which I shall never cease to despise. Let them ascend, these men whose apparent desire for altitude might make us suppose them predestined for glory, let them ascend to the most secret heights erected between the ever shaky foundations of the earth and the limpid sky spreading like a smile over a congealed swamp — perhaps they will be touched by the flight of birds who have escaped the trumpery of measure or clock (for there is no reason why such a phenomenon should not be likely to enchant them to a certain extent), but not, I can assure you, in the way that the true prophet may be struck by incendiary tiaras, he who continues on his way with his eyes closed, without concern for what is true or false, for he has arbitrarily deduced the good or bad fortune of the escapade from the dexter or sinister direction of this flight."

The vagabond reasoned thus, while on the mountain slopes the true determinants of his destiny were being materially worked out. His surges of joy and sadness, smoke and fire, yes and no, had just settled themselves on the side of the icy peak in the form of a gigantic hand made of arable land mixed with pink sandstone. Not one of the threads hanging from its tip so much as brushed against any part of this hand, whose five fingers remained outstretched in the wind, free of all contact with these long, taut strings. A short distance from this hand stood a man of very great stature, his legs wrapped in bands of white linen held in place by interwoven strips of leather whose red lattice-work stood out against the white material, replacing his tibiae, femora and muscles with a series of diamond shapes set in blood. Two fine braids of grey hair fell to his waist, parallel to the ends of his moustache which hung down like two lianas in front of his chest which was protected by a glass shield. He was a Merovingian soldier armed with a heavy axe and a hard wooden spear, whose point rose as high as the peaks of ice standing erect behind him like a sparkling trellis beneath a canopy of clouds which had gathered there to observe, in expectation of the extraordinary events which would distract them from their roving yet monotonous lives.

When the vagabond was no more than an arrow's flight from the foot of the mountain, the rocky hand suddenly closed up to form an enormous fist raised towards the sky between the stiff threads emerging from its summit. With a gesture which made his bracelets of bronze clank together with a noise more stirring than thunder, the Frankish warrior hurled his axe into the distance where it embedded itself in the very tip of the peak, opening up a deep crevasse from top to bottom. At the same time a cracking sound like that of an avalanche reverberated as far as the verdant thickets hidden in the vagabond's heart and with eyes whose pupils were iridescent like rime he saw the glass shield break into a thousand pieces while the wooden spear, slipping from the warrior's hands, came crashing down with a stormy whistling sound, severing the ropes fixed to the mountain top as it fell. This was all that was needed for a tidal wave of irony to sweep through the vagabond's soul.

Delirious with joy, he saw both warrior and fist reduced to dust, disappearing along with the severed threads and the mountain itself which soon vanished from the landscape as swiftly as the memory of a sigh when the fragrant arm of a new bend in the road envelops the gleaming limbs of the one man who uttered it.

The vagabond began walking again, and every second his step grew faster as though now he had to travel the entire world all on this same day, before the filthy backdrop of a night black yet without mystery stifled the frenetic madness of the day between its frames, built by the abject sleep of a hundred million swine…

Aurora! Aurora! Figure more pure than a spark or a sounding taken in the desert, it is your marvellous, flaming egret feathers which cause the solar vagabond's steps to quicken thus; it is your silvery dress and your blazing hair, your mouth, that pink crater from which fly your ephemeral, nonsensical words among some clinker of intelligence, and your firm, fresh hand with nails like strange, gleaming creatures that attract his head in which all that remains is a lock of blond hair! Though the roar of traffic or the clatter of pan-shaped time-pieces may shake these walls only madness could finally bring down, it is your image of fibre and flesh which comes between my eyes and every bed, destroying furniture, trinkets, loathsome tools of everyday usage and my very sanity, my disgusting sanity.

Thus between the monotonous banks of space flowed the river of the vagabond's mind which remained eternally true to itself despite its apparent contradictions. Thus it advanced, through the invariably inadequate twists and turns of language, towards the mortal ocean whose frothy bursts of laughter could never make it any less bitter.

However, a voice ordered him in vague, languorous tones to hold all this in contempt, and submitting to this one command, he forced himself to make light of it.

So choking with laughter he carried on walking. He juggled with his stick, skipped and danced. He even sang a little English ditty whose tune, comical though sentimental, was composed of notes which sparkled like minutes in the latitude where all things — even watches — catch cold. Yet his inner fate remained always with him and not one of his actions, ridiculous or touching, could make the mysterious compass marking the north of his destiny veer off course even by one millimetre.

As he was playing with his ring, throwing it up in the air and catching it again, still laughing all the while, this little mass of metal (less precious for its gold than for the delicate engraving of its rats) slipped suddenly from his grasp and fell to the ground in the middle of the path. He was already on his knees trying to recover it when he realised that it had literally *disappeared* into the ground, making a long, thin pipe which pierced the planet diagonally like a seton. Next to the mouth of this pipe the dust disturbed by the fall of the ring had formed strange reliefs in which it was possible to pick out the following words, repeated several times:

OR AUX RATS.[14]

Moreover, on a pebble protruding from the dust a few inches from this inscription the outline of an escutcheon could be seen, bisected by a vertical line which at the same time divided a feminine figure into two parts along the meridian of her mouth, navel and pubis. Although these two halves were totally different in appearance (the right half white and naked, the left half black and dressed in finery), a single banderole was spread beneath her feet, bearing the following Latin palaeontological name in raised characters similar to those which had just written OR AUX RATS:

ELEPHAS ANTIQUUS.

Hardly had the laughing man deciphered this dual summons to the subterranean passageway, a long, lugubrious tunnel hollowed out by who knows what insatiable rodents, when he felt as though he were being sucked in and, slipping down this narrow well for a few seconds or a few centuries, he was finally transported within the boundaries of a territory quite unknown to him.

Above his head whose almost perfect sphere still crowned his body (the latter supported by his feet, which in turn found themselves in the middle of a vast plain devoid of all roads and vegetation) shone a strange halo like one of Saturn's rings very close by, or a tangible zodiac. It was his ring which had expanded out of all proportion and now sat in the centre of the sky, lighting up the untrodden surface of the plain with the hairy signs of its twelve rats.

At the top of a very high tower whose battlements reached right up to the furthest dark strata of space there was a great chess-board composed of alternate matt and shiny squares. A single piece — a little figurine in the shape of a human — stood among the squares of this chess-board, but whatever its position within the quadrilateral of the game, the glaucous stars reflected in the shiny spaces put it continually into checkmate. Perhaps an observer lay hidden in the bowels of the tower calculating the consequences of this hopeless defeat, but even if he had noticed him the vagabond would not have concerned himself with this invisible player, for his attention was directed elsewhere, solicited by quite another object in a stormy setting suggested by the heavy clouds streaked with red which loomed over it.

It was a feudal castle half in ruins which stood on the distant horizon diametrically opposite the point in space occupied by the chess-board in relation to the vagabond, and despite the distance it was possible to make out the zodiacal reflection of one of the twelve rats on its crenellated walls.

The sight of this little castle (standing in the centre of a town whose ramparts had all but collapsed) soon restored the vagabond to the calm, lucid state of mind which he had lost a short time before in a maze of endless Sundays. Abandoning his untimely manifestations of false joy he gripped his stick tightly in his right hand and set off on foot towards the castle with firm, measured steps, all the while humming the following refrain in a tone which was neither particularly happy nor sad, but as indifferent as the departure of an ice-floe of fish:

I have a sweetheart whose name is Dora,
But I love Diana too, and Anna, and Flora,
Weep, chimney, weep for Aurora!

If Dora kissed me, I should kiss her too,
But she never kisses me and I stay on tip-toe.
Weep, chimney, weep for Aurora!

If Diana were a cloud, so should I be a log
Burning with a great smoke up to this nice cloud.
Weep, chimney, weep for Aurora!

If Anna were Flora, oh! could I love Flora?
If Flora were Anna, oh! could I love Anna?
Weep, chimney, weep for Aurora!

But if Dora were Diana, were Anna, were Flora, were Dora,
Oh! How wonderfully I might kiss Dora!
Weep, chimney, weep for Aurora![15]

Towards the end of this same day — while the vagabond was making his way towards the ruins of the medieval castle where he would doubtless find shelter for the night — on the other side of the world in a town where the window panes all bore the mark of a sooty thumbprint, when the setting sun could penetrate only the upper storeys of the tallest houses and the inhabitants of this coastal town, safely cloistered at home, savoured by the light of cheap candles the latest details regarding a recent rail disaster (in this case the derailment of the Orient Express just outside Vienna, the accident occurring at the very moment when one of the passengers, a famous racing driver, having told an interviewer in the same carriage how his car had overturned at top speed when a long, female hair had become caught in one of its hubs, was about to disclose the name of the woman to whom this hair belonged), thirty barrels of blood and urine hurtled down the main road towards the port and, colliding 84 times with one of the quayside bollards, thereby struck midnight 7 times over. Then the biggest barrel steadied itself as best it could, letting the other 29 stack themselves up on top of it in descending order of volume, so that in a few seconds quite a tall column had formed, narrower at the top than at the base and full of bulges like those which swell the trunks of certain tropical trees. Then through the thirty mouths of their thirty bungs, each pointing in a different direction so that the effect was that of a fountain, they unleashed the pungent liquid with which they were filled, while the smallest and consequently highest barrel spouted the following in a very shrill tone:

"QUESTION:

Which is it better to be, immaculately turned out or hanged, drawn and quartered?[16]

ANSWER:

It is better to be immaculately turned out than to be hanged, drawn and quartered, because he who is immaculately turned out still has time to be hanged, drawn and quartered, but he who is hanged, drawn and quartered has no time left to be immaculately turned out.

"FOR WHICH REASON we are putting the famous furniture of Descartes up for sale at absolutely unbeatable prices, starting with his *stove*, which some say was merely a room sufficiently heated to allow his mind to reach the moderate temperature (neither scorching nor freezing, but simply that of lukewarm water) necessary to guarantee his thoughts their maximum efficiency, and finishing with his illustrious *tabula rasa* which, in order to give it greater value than whistling to raise the dead in a cemetery recently given over to market gardening, he should first have stripped of its four legs — the only procedure which would have allowed him in all honesty to call it a 'shorn table'.[17]

"When a physicist, eager to complete the framework within which in his opinion the universe had been placed from the beginning of time, invented the expression *absolute zero*, a point he located at minus 273 degrees Centigrade on the thermometric scale, he did not understand the symbolic value of the conjunction of these two terms which his mouth had uttered, nor that he was thus declaring, like a prophetess in a trance unaware of the profound significance of her words, the indisputable identity of the absolute with nothingness.

"At a time when relationships are cracking and disintegrating like bundles of dead wood, it is not a fantastic funeral pyre which is being prepared and whose flames will illuminate life now stripped of all its contingent dustbins by a ghastly rag-and-bone man with a satanically svelte body, but rather a hearth of dead ashes, swept away by the first gust of wind so that nothing remains and a hypothetical witness perched on an imaginary knoll in order to observe at leisure the outcome of this event can only pronounce this single sentence: 'It is absolute nudity.'

"As soon as the moment has passed when gloves and garments hollow themselves out with a view to admitting the bodily substance which nests in their cavities, tear off your clothes, you men and women dressed up for ludicrous dances, rip up your shoes, stamp on your hats, shed your skin, your muscles, your skeletons, your desires and your ideas, unload yourselves like tip-carts full of stones whose contents fall out block by block with a thunderous roar, tear even these stones apart and their last pieces of rubble, so that the absolute may advance in all the wild majesty of a non-existent king, a hypothetical monarch hoisted on to this monumental rostrum to the top of which leads this zero-staircase comprising exactly 273 steps.

"To form the number composing these stairs the figure 2 was the first to appear. It is supple and well-balanced, sinuous and beautiful like a couple making love. It is the first even number, symmetry at its base, but this primordial parity can also be spelled FATHER[18] and thus become the original sign of all ignominy. It is by this *par* in the form of *pa* that we in fact arrive at 3, that waltzing figure of generation, that vaudeville number, that derisory trinity which ought never to show itself except in underpants. However, 7 stands between these two, a sickly sling of seven shades, rainbow of the plague, and if it stands there in the middle of this number it is to demonstrate that just as all the rays of the various colours result in white when superimposed, so all the numbers when mixed together merge to form 0, a circle with neither beginning nor end and thus a marvellously appropriate figure of chaos, a mass which holds neither relationships nor reality, a soft, pale ball which is in no way visible against the negative, colourless background on which your lives are and will ever remain merely positive images, black and ephemeral.

"So to give yourselves a chance to enter into such a play of mirrors and try to become their central reflection, shed your flesh, your bones, your feelings and your very thoughts, and then with stroke upon stroke of a hazardous axe hack at a pane of glass which remains eternally colourless, formless, without silvering and with no possibility of ever splintering. The monotonous string which quivers out of the range of bows bent by archers of symmetrical stature is the thin thread of the noose, the musical stave on which only nightmarish and never dreamlike *arpeggios* can be composed. If the bells ring out on feast-days and funeral nights in every town choked by sloping valleys of meat, pebbles or gall, it is so as to be heard in the far-off place where these chimerical mirrors intersect, so that this confusion of sound and vision, a confusion to be scrupulously carried into every domain (mixing up mouth and belly, touch and sex, string and heart, the spiritual and the natural), might momentarily give rise to nudity in all its whitish magnitude, the feminine phantom whose structure is as imprecise as the limestone tank concealing rubble and spiders' webs next to which you sometimes sleep with your foreheads pressed against its rough wall, believing that your heads are thus in physical and perfectly perceptible contact with your inner reality, your substance externalised in the form of this tank and suddenly set opposite you, an upside-down well or gasometer. We barrels full of blood and urine partake of this unique substance because of our cylindrical shape and our bungs, but we are merely its comical reflection, the only one you are really in a position to gaze upon...

"For you will never attain this sparkling white nudity, this charming, disdainful princess who is the object of all your desires. You will never ravish her body, though it is as real as the diabolical torment it engenders in your heads, for your nudity, your own whiteness, is less than dust and as a ground on which to prostrate yourselves could only be compared to shifting sands. You will never penetrate her mind which, free of all circles and segments, is as clear as the inside of a glass sphere, for your minds, even when rid of their bodily casing, would immediately burst once inside, fat fruit full of filthy juice which the four-dimensional mould, as heavy as air, could no longer contain. Neither will you touch her heart, for its relentless diastole and systole have absolutely nothing in common with yours, and you would be completely incapable of adapting your rhythm to its beat, a movement which pumps no blood but is only the vague and oh so distant pulsating of frozen foam in a motionless silence.

"You see it is as little for you as it is for absurd philosophy that she is constructed, this fantastic carcass this disconcerting carnal figure born of the obscure movements of space and the encounter of nickel-plated projectiles on the as yet unwarped surface of time and destiny. If it happened that for a brief moment she deigned to appear before your eyes, by chance in a dream or in the maze of a mortal miasma, then perhaps it would be in the fleeting guise of a magnificent naked magician with an abundance of hair like a wild beast but with several wide rings of burnished copper encircling her body. Her shoulders, whiter and more matt than lunar wax, protrude from this inadequate armour which also allows her breasts to show through, as hard and equal as the Magdeburg hemispheres. Her stomach, firm and rounded like the trajectory described by a fruit when the rebellious wind catapults it from the tree where it had hung like a dead man's jaw, is as attractive as her rump, cut in two by a deep gorge from which only crows and vultures would fly, were it possible for a few living creatures to have built nests there with branches torn from the cypress trees of cemeteries or with tiny pieces of stone taken from the ruins of a mausoleum. As for her head, that beautiful standard of soft and delicate skin planted at the top of this strange set of muscles, it wears a hat made of a narrow semicircle of bluish metal, bearing, by way of a crest, a very tall icy peak shaped like a lightning conductor. This gleaming rod which soars up from the middle of her forehead transforms her into an ancient unicorn, but a unicorn whose sharp pickaxe attacks not only the bark of trees and wild beasts, but also men, nature, the sky and the universe, because being of steel, this stake communicates with the storm.

"It is thus, fatally armed with this eternal spike — a pale needle magnetically attracted to the pole of pain and torture, a slender shaft reduced to an ethereal single line — that just once, perhaps, you will fleetingly glimpse her image when you are nothing but lunulae squashed between the twin shields of nothingness and the absolute, crushed at their precise tangential point, and when unlike today the world no longer spreads out its pages, blackened with letters and numbers, with a view to displaying what odious advertisement?"

At this point the barrel-orator stopped speaking, for already the jets of organic liquid spurted less violently from the bungs and became mere trickles slowly oozing out, until finally their resonant brassy-red flow ceased altogether.

When the very last drop had been absorbed by the ground and the flow of blood and urine, like the high-pitched flow of eloquence before it, had entirely dried up, the column of philosophising casks collapsed all at once with the lugubrious and cavernous sound of a pile of falling coffins, and the thirty barrels scattered, all rolling into the sea where one by one they were snatched by various currents which carried them off to the four corners of the Earth, dihedral angles cut in a pure frost of abstraction by the knife, itself abstract, forming the fin of a phantom fish.

Meanwhile in the town a very young prostitute was mysteriously dying in a sleazy tavern; two officials dressed in black were stripping her body which was bedecked with the liquid silk usually constituting the red blazon of murdered women, and upon her still trembling breast, as white as snow for it was powdered with cocaine, they found a half-faded tattoo of a medieval castle whose outer walls, dominating an enormous, disquieting lagoon, were none other than the ramparts of this selfsame town, a town which had remained very beautiful owing to its name, the sound of which was both bitter and fresh:

AIGUES-MORTES.[19]

A few steps higher on the atmospheric staircase, where birds are no longer supported by the too rarefied air and are obliged to use their claws instead of their wings, like explorers hanging from the walls of a crater, the indescribable dress and flaming scarves attached to the network of lightning which now composed the transformed substance of Aurora fluttered in the sky like strips of flesh, while the last flounces of her vaporous skirt spread out as far as the horizon in the shape of a fan, a narrow triangle of material which could easily have been eliminated by a single gust of wind.

Inside the still too robust framework of this triangular fabric made of an amalgam of clouds and crystals, Aurora was bored to death, and behind the mercurial bars formed by the intermittent density of the void, the lions of this painful boredom yawned at the thunderstorms and roared.

A suffocating heat filled huge carts with blocks of its summer-coloured ore. Deep in a forest whose trees had not yet sacrificed their bark to the sculpture of coal, a thawing pond was letting its jewels melt, shaped like the skeletons of the fish which for several months it had held prisoner. The cold, that enemy of wasps and mosquitoes, had now fled and gone to ground in a region of extinct lava from which basalt is extracted for use by the sculptors of a barefaced lie. However, through these multiple veins thickened by torpor several glowing-red pins circulated, carried along by a clear, bright blood still flowing despite the weight of uncertainty whose false units accumulated, piled up one on top of the other by left hands and right hands whose thin, sinuous forms collided without respite in a contest of contrasting, contrasted, contrary and contradictory lines…

# VI.

The sun had only just gone down behind the dark blue line of the sea when the vagabond, who had been walking continuously for many a long hour, arrived at the gates of an ancient town whose endless fortifications extended along a vast beach interspersed with ponds, marshes and pot-holes, a beach condemned from the very beginning to the treachery of soft sludge and quicksand. This was Aigues-Mortes, a deserted town abandoned since the day the king who had built it died of the plague during a mad and criminal crusade. Aigues-Mortes, which obstinate geographers stubbornly persist in situating on the northern shore of the Mediterranean, even though today this port, described as once flourishing, displays its crumbling quays and cracked walls beside an infinitely heavier and saltier sea whose boundaries may only be discovered by looking on the back of a map of the world, a sea which is bordered in the South by the Black River but in the North by Mont Blanc.

Continuing his journey, the vagabond went through the gates of the city and quickly became aware of its deserted state, exploring its empty, lifeless streets where there were neither shops nor houses and whose gloomy drains all converged upon the half-ruined feudal castle which he had first noticed towards midday, but which in the end he found to be nothing but a long hangar made of mouldy planks with a tarpaulin roof torn in several places and consequently not at all suited to doing battle with the elements.

A little to the east of the town the rumblings of a still vague and distant storm could be heard, in clouds still too ill-defined to be clearly distinguished from the falling darkness, but with every second this storm drew imperceptibly nearer, advancing with such regularity that it was already possible to forecast the exact moment when it would sit directly above the vagabond's head — and above mine too, for at the same time as the eternal walker was entering the precincts of the town, taking care to avoid the reptiles slumbering among its stones, I was also arriving there, having taken a completely different route which I had followed for several days, despite never having had the slightest idea where it would lead.

I observed the vagabond and this strange shed (which it seemed was to provide shelter for the final and also most concrete form of his destiny) with acute, alveolar attention far more organic than the usual course of any cerebral manœuvre, and with stares as prolonged as pine needles or slender plant stalks — I, who indeed seemed to have been reduced to playing the miserable role of spectator, despite the protests of my arms thrashing the air like oars, my restless legs and my mouth gross with sarcasm regarding the abject fate which I had thus been dealt.

The planks forming the fake castle were extremely knotty and the rich colour of damp earth, and their eddying lines grew wider like the circular furrows ploughed in a fallow field by the fall of a very heavy stone dropped from a sufficiently high atmospheric point for it to pierce the earth, stirring the soil like the surface of a lake, before sinking for ever into the subterranean glue.

The vagabond certainly did not waste his time searching these planks, identical to the one I had used as a kind of raft at the outset of this journey, to see if they bore a sign of any importance to him (a mass of lines and dots, harsh and smooth surfaces, a rough, rugged figure resembling what creature, what thorny rose of imagination or fact?), for without hesitation he entered the hangar before even the smallest drop of rain falling from clouds which grew every second more numerous had prompted him to find shelter, however pitiful.

As soon as he was inside, the scene changed… I remained standing outside, more than ever conscious of the sinister sartorial rags making still heavier the weight of my human reality, all magic seeming quite dead for me that day, and all I could do was press my face against the thin partition of wood, one eye level with the narrow space separating two planks, in order to use for purposes of observation the transparency of this diaphanous aerial medium, this gap intersecting the opacity of two thicker substances, while inside the hangar the vagabond once again became the only actor on stage.

The shed was an extremely long construction, a sort of interminable corridor leading to a very small door opposite another very distant one through which the vagabond had entered. On the floor there was no trace of furniture, except for one stool close to the entrance in the shape of a truncated cone hewn from black wood whose circular, superimposed veins were all on a plane parallel with the base of the cone. The vagabond sat down on this seat and looked around him.

The dusty walls were half those of an inn, half those of a castle. The whole of the right side was covered by a long tapestry, patched and very threadbare, whose fringes had been gnawed by the teeth of mice and rats yet whose colours were still vivid enough to enable the onlooker to make out what it had once depicted: gryphons, chimeras, wyverns, salamanders, unicorns and all kinds of fantastic creatures gathered round a tree whose petrified fruits, slightly egg-shaped, looked more like Easter gifts than diving masks. On the left side there hung a large number of illustrations.

First, an advertisement for "Johnnie Walker" whisky, with the picture of a gentleman with short side-whiskers dressed in a red jacket from the days of the last stage-coaches and wearing white breeches, turned-down boots and a grey top hat, with a switch in his hand. In the distant background his rival the White Horse was galloping unbridled in a hunt, having probably unseated his rider at the last river jump.

Next (after several notices recommending all kinds of products) came an Italian landscape with a barefoot Neapolitan woman in the foreground and on the horizon the smoking crater of Vesuvius. A broken column pompously recalled the time and the disaster, but despite this the peasant woman still carried a full basket of fresh fruit perched jauntily on her head.

Then came a snow-covered steppe across which a sledge was being pulled by a pack of large dogs all foaming at the mouth, while behind them a multitude of wolves' eyes gleamed wickedly, luminous fangs piercing their first prey of darkness.

Finally, following these banal images remarkable only for their skies painted a strange shade which changed every time one looked at them, there was a rather more curious print fixed to the wall with four nails whose heads shone brightly despite the rust eating them away. This depicted a very young girl of perhaps fourteen or fifteen dressed in a short lace slip. The ornamental pattern perforating her stockings culminated in spearheads, and at her neck there hung a small cross whose branches were fingers bleeding lightly under the nail. She was sitting at a sewing-machine by an open window through which a rocky Rhenish landscape was visible, and on the cloth she was stitching the following motto could be read, embroidered in Gothic lettering:

Verstörung
das hübsche Schulmädchen[20]

The vagabond stared at this picture for a very long time, for it attracted him more than all the rest owing to the beauty of the young girl, the elegance of her long plaits and the great delicacy of the inscription. Thus, once again, a shimmering necklace of sentimental stones had become his only toy, to the exclusion of all the other objects surrounding him.

Outside, the thundery rain began to crash down with the sound of broken glass, but the eyes and ears of the tramp registered nothing of this — not the torrents of water, not the darkness which was now almost total, not the sky locked away behind the bolted clouds, not the violent flashes of lightning relentlessly following one after the other while no one but myself could have known what they in fact were: actual fragments of the delicate complexion worn by Aurora now that she had changed into lightning.

Leaning against the wall of planks which formed the very body of the hangar, I listened to the rumbling thunder without being able to determine whether this obscure sound concealed any intelligible words. I admired the breathtaking lightning, whether broken lines or bursts of sparks like shocks of hair (also capable of crackling if combed when the air is full of electricity), which, impeded by invisible obstacles in the air, propagated itself in each of these forms in turn, and I thought of Aurora, of her blinding reality now revealed to me in the sad dazzle of a limitless but consequently impossible love, a terrible sign of fire whose dry burning will in the end consume me to my very bones. Weary of my pitiful role on which not even the palest light was shed by this strange but too distant creature born, on a day of diluvial despair, in one of the bitterest recesses of what is generally called my brain, I watched the vagabond, the only living being with me at that moment within the walls of Aigues-Mortes, but with every second my eyes grew wilder and less clear, so impatient was I to see an end to all this phantasmagoria.

Behind the lagoon the sea murmured ever-identical phrases which were broken up and blurred by foam, but even so I could just about distinguish these words interrupted by Aurora's muffled explosions:

The flax of thought (the flax of thought)
the mild meadow of a mouth with moist contours (the flax of thought)
at the hour when the raven hollows out (the flax of thought)
its silent ravine (the flax of thought)
this hair of nameless smoke (the flax of thought)
more devious (the flax) than a serpent's heart (the flax of thought)
like a garden of the blind (the flax the flax of thought)
the red curve of a mouth closes itself up (the flax of thought)
shuts away the white harrow (the flax) of the flax of thought
shiny as a snowy tomb (the flax the flax the flax of thought)
on the balcony of slumber the madwoman laughed like a comet
KNEES when we locked you away.

However much I repeated this pathetic song I could summon neither violence nor melancholy to colour the sight before me, and despite the growing storm, Aurora's rage or love which I still hoped would destroy the world with its thunderbolts, nothing stirred inside the hangar, neither the roof nor even the walls made of planks which had seemed so close to collapse.

All of a sudden, however, with malicious pleasure because I deduced that at long last perhaps something was going to happen, I saw the vagabond get up, leaving the truncated cone on which he had been sitting to point its non-existent tip towards the ceiling, then walk towards the door at the far end of the hangar, and just then I noticed that two objects which I had not seen before were attached to this door: a blonde wig with divinely flowing locks as sweet as the contents of a honeycomb and, hanging next to it, a white silk night-dress still moulded to the shape of a very beautiful woman's body.

The vagabond could only advance with great difficulty, for the atmosphere had become extremely viscous owing to the magnetic effluence with which it was charged now that the clouds had reached their maximum concentration. Using his hands he pushed his way through thick drapery, a whole panoply of flags whose material and poles conspired to hamper his progress. He walked slowly as if through a thick fog, like the breaker of a magic safe piercing the grey wall of people deliberately obstructing his passage. He could only put one foot very slowly in front of the other, but despite this annoying sluggishness the final resolution was not long in coming.

As soon as the tramp, having finally reached his destination, placed his hand on the brass knob controlling this minute door (leading to who knows what marvellous recess?), the faded tapestry all along the right side of the hangar suddenly tore in half. At the same moment an ominously coloured lightning flash appeared and the entire universe shuddered, moved to its furthest fibres by a cry of delirious purity which came from a woman's throat more taut and curved than any plant, even a poisonous one… And as the vagabond's eardrums burst, their membranes torn apart by the tremendous peal of thunder which rang out simultaneously, the lightning struck him directly on the forehead, slid straight down his skeleton, spread through his whole body, pricking it as though with a thousand needles, and then escaped through his ten fingers in the form of a spray of golden egret plumes, a fleeting bouquet stemming from the electric power of Aurora. Then every cavity in his body became enlarged, like stone caves whose vaults are struck for the first time by the gleaming torches and humming voices of explorers, a steel spring relaxed then instantly coiled back up inside each of his arteries, and the world caved in.

Yet while the external scenery still remained in place in front of the dim lanterns of the stars which act as footlights on its grubby boards, I could see, from the *rigor mortis* which was already beginning to take hold of him, that the vagabond, dying a most natural death, had just put on the sharp skis of vertigo, so that at the precise moment when in the vast snowfield so ardently coveted he became a tiny black speck among Aurora's myriad flakes, I was not surprised to observe that on his earthly forehead now hard and white like marble, a gravestone hoisted above the cemetery which had always been his body, a name seemingly that of a woman was inscribed. I thought it would be AURORA, the tender name of her whose love was always going to kill him just as at last he was on the point of touching her, but approaching the corpse I found that the engraved letters did not all correspond to the syllables of this name. For this word (traced by the beak of an insufficiently prophetic bird or else produced by a slip of the dark lips of space), this word was armed with an H like the spasm of a hiccup as well as with the two Rs which make the thunder of anguish roll, and this term, derived from some sort of decadent, barbaric Latin, was spelled:

HORRORA.

Many years ago the entire city of Aigues-Mortes had been plunged into perpetual darkness, a night as thick as black coffee, and beside its walls a hideous fortune-teller shuffled her cards, she who always confuses ALWAYS with NEVER, never NEVER with ALWAYS, and can only pronounce "baby's cry" as "the end is nigh," so rotten are her teeth.

I reflected on what I had seen and, watching the pole-star glinting softly like the ironic point of the two-edged sword of Paracelsus above the hangar now transformed into a charnel-house, I contemplated the name Aurora, inextricably linked to the destiny of this astonishing girl who was now being carried off by the last shreds of cloud towards a skyscraper constructed (from what immutable cement?) on the edge of a continent obscure yet extraordinarily light and enduring, and I remembered that in Latin the word *hora* means "hour", that the stem *or* is found in *os*, *oris* which means "mouth" or "orifice", that it was on Mount *Ararat* that the Ark came to rest after the Flood and finally, that if Gérard de Nerval hanged himself one night in a back street of central Paris, then it was because of two semi-spectral creatures each of whom bore half of this name: Aurelia and Pandora.

The storm had completely abated, and I was cloaked in the darkness of a night which was now very still and as black as soot, forming a veritable shroud (as long as this last word is seen less as the name of a whitish material than as that of a dark cloth serving simply to wipe away the sweat of the dead). The stars were only twinkling faintly in their Machiavellian combinations of attraction, hanging and repulsion, but to light my way there was the incandescence of the sea, teeming with a mass of microscopic animals covering everything with their rays. The shifting sands, the ponds, the marshes and the pot-holes all lay dormant, withdrawn from the outside world like anchorites in their miry silence, and no glint of light betrayed their relentless slumber, for the cesspool of the world, though partially negated by the halo of phosphorescent waves, blackened everything with its buboes.

Not a single cry rose up from anywhere; still less the sound of clocks. Not one human murmur, no swishing of wing or fin, no sound of burrowing mole or screech of rat being strangled in a trap, no rustling of a tree, no friction of stone on stone or meeting of canal and stream and no sigh prolonging the creak of a shadowy door being opened came to collapse at my ears like an exhausted messenger sent on its sonorous journey by the external world. Apart from the gentle rustle as the different materials of the various layers of my clothing brushed against each other in compliance with my movements, I could no longer hear anything at all, not even the last (and now too distant) claps of thunder from the dying storm, and not even the final repercussions of the disturbance in the air created by Aurora's phenomenal scream. Everything was drowned in silence, muffled in gelatin. The unwearying universe persisted in sleeping soundly, undisturbed in its mediocrity. No scar of past storms made any impression on its insensitive skin. A slight movement to and fro, perhaps from its outer shell pitching and rolling on the feeble, colourless waves of an incurable eternity, served only to deepen its sleep, just as that of a new-born infant is enhanced when its parents — worse than criminals in their fond belief that this is an act of tenderness — rock the cradle instead of asphyxiating the child.

I had to begin to understand that no cataclysm would strike with its bludgeon of ether and lay waste the tainted cathedral that towered above underground crypts, hiding-places even more secret than those of matter, and that I would for ever be tied to the stake of inevitably secondary ideas, for nothing if not this destruction of the world could free me from the dripping creel whose interwoven canes had encircled me, like wire netting around a prisoner, at the moment when the witch of birth had given me life in spite of myself, throwing me body and soul into the cogs of this awful machine with the aid of an ephemeral seed.

So the guillotine of the universe would remain standing with its red posts intact. Impossible to escape its implacable round hole since, by means of the two parallel lines between which this circle is placed, rational omnipotence openly affirms its intention of continuing to reign supreme in its geometrical pallor, more repulsive than a crystal carafe eternally filled with stale, insipid water.

This was how I interpreted the lesson of silence, and I was endeavouring to make the skin of my eardrums as thin as possible, so that they might vibrate on contact with the slightest sound, when at two opposite points of the globe — one in the East, the other in the West — a weak tremor occurred.

These two disturbances, intervening just as I recognised that there was no longer any hope that the world would end, or that there would be some upheaval whose hammering lightning would be capable of crushing relationships until their blood ran — these two minor dips in the uniformly level steppe (relieved only by the lichen of boredom whose stuccoed branches creep into the hopelessly hollow moulds of absent events) instantly inflated me with a fluid lighter than the one which swells the envelope of a hot-air balloon, till suddenly disappointment struck me like a bolt of lightning, bursting my ridiculous rotundity and discarding it wrinkled like the skin of an old woman and imprisoned me once again in the mesh of a net. For as soon as I had determined the true nature of the two accidents in question, I was forced, as if bound hand and foot, to face the facts and tell myself that the battle was lost once and for all.

On one side of the world, where the sun sets, the sea swelled with wide concentric circles which overcame the waves and gradually put an end to the phosphorescent phenomena. On the other side, where the sun rises, a great mass of swirling sand had formed and was advancing like a thick column, gradually filling the horizon with its whiteness striped with black grooves which led up to the cable-moulding of its capital, sculptured in dust.

When the aquatic turbulence had reached its full extent and the diameter of the largest circle was roughly equal to the distance from the shore to the horizon, a bright red dot came slowly into sight, marking the exact centre of the whirlpool with a bloody spot which was at first indistinct like a piece of coral but then became as clear and sharply defined as the red of a Phrygian cap carried on the end of a pike. This coloured pivot seemed to rule the concentric waves and appeared long to have been the cause of their movement, even when this was still invisible, but it remained a spot for only a few moments and then, having emerged completely from the water, showed itself to be something quite other than a pivot. The red dot was in fact merely crowning a long white figure covered in seaweed and coral, emaciated by the sea salt and made brown by a sun of mud, a tentacular mass whose rays use the shells buried there by formless animals as the vehicle of their muddy light. This figure grew visibly bigger by the minute, absorbing one by one the circular eddies on which it almost seemed to feed, and soon its great ghostly body towered in the air on two long legs hidden by the pouches of a sort of white tunic. At the same time the whirlpool disappeared and the circular blistering gradually flattened out. Thus the circumferences nearest the centre were consumed by the figure, while those on the periphery vanished of their own accord, progressively eliminated by the levelling of their contours, so that after a while the white apparition crested with red commanded a completely flat expanse — a marine mirror in whose mathematical nakedness I could then recognise, standing draped in what was left of his priestly garb, the figure of Damocles Siriel.

As this murderous hierarch emerged from the abyss of the sea which hundreds of years before had swallowed him up, a no less intriguing phenomenon was occurring on dry land — someone else fleeing from limbo, but this time from a subterranean limbo.

Thus a column of sand had advanced from the East, and on its whitish background the parallel black streaks were visible which, like rails, steered the gaze towards its overhanging volutes. When this pillar was sufficiently close and the sand forming it suitably compact, the column appeared as a solid structure, erasing even the memory of the swirling mass of sand which had generated it. On the column's light-coloured screen the vertical black lines danced about and intermingled like shadows projected on to the ground by the bars of railings when two runners carrying lamps rush towards each other and pass, both having followed a straight line parallel to the railings but in opposite directions. This criss-crossing of dark lines, intersecting and then returning very briefly to their original positions, went on until the movements of the imaginary runners caused them to group themselves into a more important figure whose principal features were as follows: on the upper part of the column a sort of enormous black V formed by a large number of lines almost exactly superimposed (the very sharp point of the V indicating that here they had coincided perfectly, but the two ascending sides which both grew gradually thicker showing that after this point of absolute convergence the lines had begun slightly to diverge), and lower down, on the bottom part of the shaft, two thin black lines positioned vertically one on either side, like the outline which in a drawing distinguishes an object from the surrounding page.

When this figure had attained a certain stability the column again moved perceptibly nearer, and I saw that it was on its way to meet the ghost of Damocles Siriel which was now walking on the lagoon in the direction of the old hangar made of planks inside which lay the remains of the vagabond. The two moving objects met up at the door of this building, and now the column was so close to me that I could see the black lines marking it were none other than the black silk V and the two parallel lines of the same material forming the lapels and trouser stripes of the light-coloured garment for tropical evenings which had once been the distinctive costume of the man in the white dinner-jacket. A rust-coloured stain recalled the fresh rose whose surprising flesh had previously adorned his buttonhole, and two gleaming black pebbles at the base of the column shone like the perfectly smooth skin of two very elegant shoes of patent leather. As for the complicated volutes of the sculptured capital, they could only be identified as the ravaged, bitten face surmounting the body of the man who had long ago sunk down to the mysterious substrata of sand called Base-of-the-Desert, while in front of him the volcanic metamorphoses took place of a pyramid tinged with blood and flames.

Now united, having just emerged from their murky depths, the two ghosts silently entered the hangar, their clothes filthy and full of holes, bearing the marks of deep burns which had devoured them — latent fires of cupriferous ore, or else the sickly-sweet saliva of ground swells, both torturers more efficient than the fiercest of furnaces — as they rotted in the blackness of their distant exiles under the multiple layers of earth and sea.

Lying on the ground beneath the poor shelter of the tarpaulin, shreds of which — all that remained after the violent ravages of the storm — covered only part of the hangar, the vagabond's corpse continued to stiffen, arms in at its sides and legs apart, its ghastly pallor and frozen flesh reminiscent of a statue without a plinth made in the image of torture victims. There was nothing left of his two stout shoes except a few hobnails which studded the ground nearby. The threads of his coarse clothing had completely disintegrated. Entirely naked, the corpse lay on its back, the fingers of its right hand clasped around the cover of a book whose pages had almost all been burnt, but on the stony cartouche of its forehead it was still possible to make out the inscription which lips of lightning had traced with their fiery graver just before a more piercing and icy embrace.

Without undue caution, Damocles Siriel and the man in the white dinner-jacket seized the corpse. Lifting it like a wooden beam they took it out of the hangar, one of them holding its head, the other its feet. Then, once outside Aigues-Mortes, they found themselves back on the deserted lagoon and, still carrying their load, they walked on for a considerable distance.

The wind danced languorously round their ghostly ears, but it was no longer possible to fit words to the tune whistled by the sea in an infernally tedious monotone, for Aurora had ascended for ever into the scudding clouds which were driven by her torment. Above them shone the moon's transparent horn, curved like the glass bend in an alchemist's retort, while the stars scrawled their amazing magic across the sky. Damocles Siriel and the man in the white dinner-jacket walked slowly onwards, seeming almost unaware of their macabre cargo whose already opaque eyes sparkled very faintly like the secretions of two strange molluscs.

Arriving at the largest and most foul-smelling swamp, the two ghosts stopped. They dumped their burden on an expanse of wet yellow sand, and now that the spectres found themselves face to face their eyes met for a moment. Then in hushed tones they exchanged a few words, a conversation of which I caught only snatches:

"… to end with a clear-sighted flight…"

"… the need for a wall…"

"… escalope and entrails…"

"… soften the vulture's claws…"

"… it could be any minute now…"

"… absurd…"

"… yes, but perhaps…"

"… putrid path."

Their confabulation over, without further ado they rolled up the dirty sleeves of their tattered clothes, picked up the corpse again and then, after energetically swinging it in the air for a while, they flung it as high and as far as they could towards the middle of the swamp.

First the body whistled up into the air like an arrow. For a second it remained suspended in mid-air, then it fell head first and sank up to the hips into the brownish sludge of the swamp. Its mouth and ears instantly filled with mud while its legs, which stayed afloat because they were still wide apart, continued to point towards the zenith as taut in appearance as the two prongs of a catapult when, its projectile released, the angle of its Y subtends the firmament.

Despite the gears of the wind, the teeth of the salt and the knives of the sun, the vagabond's corpse remained in this immutable half-buried position for an eternity, its head and body directed towards a subterranean existence. For an eternity the dead man remained thus, a prey to the rain and the tides, and Damocles Siriel had long since disappeared along with the man in the white dinner-jacket — returning to their hidden burial places by the same route which had brought them — when the bones of the corpse were silently laid bare. One by one the cells of its flesh fell away, strewing the ground all around it with their powdery plaster. Boils had doubtless formed on its mottled gums and the inscription itself must surely have faded, its hollow letters filled up with mud more solid than mortar. In the town, the hangar now consisted merely of one worm-eaten plank, the stale air stank and the sea's waves, whose foam was turning mouldy, were now nothing more than mushroom-beds. Only its shin-bones still pointed rigidly upwards, for their accursed fork was to outlast all this decay.

Gloomily I surveyed this scene, only too aware that it had existed for centuries, and I became more and more desperately bored... Now I had really had enough of all this! It was eternally unchanging; no miraculous explosion set it alight. Curses spurted from my mouth along with obscenities, imprecations and spittle. I had to get out of this place at all costs, yet I was fixed to the spot like a stake.

Countless seasons passed. I had the time to witness almost a thousand storms, all of them sham, whose worst lightning was no more irritating than a mosquito. The walls of Aigues-Mortes were eventually reduced entirely to ruins and the day even came when they were rebuilt. Drainage work eliminated the shifting sands and the swamps. A concrete dyke concealed the menacing legs of the vagabond behind its wall. Several major shipping routes brought the mummified sea back to life, picked its mushrooms and transformed them poetically into jellyfish. A luxurious hotel was constructed on the site of the mysterious hangar, and a wealthy industrial community grew up.

It was after this that, leaving the most magnificently lit gaming-room of a gilded casino which had opened on the beach that very night, and turning up the collar of my large, English-style overcoat against the chill of the night air, I lit up a fragrant cigar with one flick of my lighter and walked towards the sea.

I passed a few courting couples out for a stroll. I heard their hands brushing against each other, their short, light-hearted words and their suppressed laughter. Too absorbed in their own conversations, they paid no attention to what I was doing. Distant orchestras playing ridiculous tunes only infuriated me all the more.

So when I reached the water's edge and the foam of the lapping waves began to damage the tips of my shoes, I did not stop. Without slowing down even slightly, taking care simply to put out my cigar whose scattered ash merged with the sand, I walked calmly into the sea.

The last sounds from the casino, the clink of fortune in the roulette wheel, the flight of bewildered birds driven mad by the light, the sad farewells of those who were to be separated for ever by the infinity of a night, the horns of cars travelling at top speed beside the railway tracks, the puffing of locomotives condemned slavishly to follow utilitarian parallel lines — all these noises assaulted my ears as I went slowly down the sandy slope, each step plunging me a little deeper into the sea.

When the water had risen to my neck, my feet left the ground of their own accord and rose to the surface like weightless bottle-imps, while my head stayed above water, so that I found myself floating aimlessly on my back like a tired swimmer taking a rest.

This horizontal position resembling that of an arrow in flight made me the plaything of all the currents. Low tides carried me out to sea, sweeping my body along like a block of ice. Flotsam of flesh and blood, a human raft, I was tossed about by every ocean. Birds pecked my face and fish struck my sides with their gills, while others stroked me with their scaly fan-shaped fins. The unseeing blades of bloodthirsty propellers brushed past my hands.

At last, after a long and exhausting journey, I arrived one fine morning in the estuary of the Seine. Although against the current, I swam upstream, past Rouen, Vernon, Bonnières, Saint-Cloud and heaven knows how many other towns! I had set out to return to the source. However, the weight of my sodden clothing was now such that my journey had to end, having lost its initial impetus.

One winter day I stopped at Notre-Dame bridge. My numb body, heavy with cold, came to a halt against one of the large metal rings hanging from the stone riverbank. Drowning the mournful noise I made as I collided with this monstrous piece of chain, a tugboat's siren carved a mirror from the sky and revealed the state I was in:

on my chest the last leaf to fall with its unserrated edges was rotting like a red heart;

on the little finger of my left hand the band of my *de luxe* cigar sat like a ring, and although its prolonged immersion in the water had partially erased its colours, I could read in tarnished gold on a faded red background:

O'RORA

LARGE TOWER BLOCK LACQUERED WHITE

IN THE UNITED STARS OF AMER-TIC

Further away from me, quite high up on the right, was the cathedral spire of Notre-Dame to which my glazed stare was riveted. This temple was built by neither Semiramis nor the Queen of Sheba, but they say that on its stones are engraved the principal secrets of Nicolas Flamel, more enigmatic even than those of Paracelsus.

. . . . . . . . . . . . . . . . . . . . . . . . . . . . . . . . . . . . . . . . . . . . . . . . . . . . . . . . . . . . .

1927-1928.

## NOTES

1. In the original *Le Petit Poucet*, i.e. Tom Thumb. In the French tradition, Perrault's fairy story equates with the Anglo-Saxon version of "Hansel and Gretel".
2. Literally: "staircase wit", meaning a witty riposte only thought of after the original occasion.
3. Leiris writes *ils les emmerdent*, the figurative meaning of which is: "to hell with them!" or "damn them!"
4. The effect of this alliterative play on words is impossible to convey in translation. Literal equivalents are as follows:

   *moi*: me, *mythe*: myth, *mie*: beloved, or breadcrumb, *merde!*: shit!, *mue*: moulting, *mort*: dead, or death.

   *je mords*: I bite, *je murais*: I was walling up, *je m'ourdis*: I wove myself in, *je m'ordonnerai*: I will order myself, *je muserais*: I would muse, *que je m'use*: that I wear myself out, *mortel*: mortal, or fatal, *amour*: love.
5. La Place de Grève was a Parisian square on the banks of the Seine which was once the site of criminal executions. *La grève* means a sandy shore or strand.
6. The song is rhymed in the original.
7. *Eau* is French for "water", *rho* (ρ) is the seventeenth letter of the Greek alphabet and with the name *Râh*, this rebus is a homonym of "Au-ro-ra".
8. This translates literally as "will have gold", *or* being French for "gold". The first syllable of "Aurora" and *Aura* (Au) is the chemical symbol of gold (Latin *aurum*).
9. *Pierre* (stone) is also the French equivalent of the Christian name Peter.
10. "Infernal stone" is an old name for lunar caustic.
11. The French *Hors des guenilles Œil de la mort!* is a poetic gloss on the word *orgueil* (pride).
12. This refrain is rhymed in the original.
13. In French *égaux* (equal) is a homonym of the word *ego*.
14. Literally "gold to the rats", and in French another homonym of "Au-ro-ra".
15. This entire song is in English in the original.
16. In French, a pun on the similar literal sense of the idioms *tiré à quatre épingles* (pulled apart by four pins), and *tiré à quatre chevaux* (pulled [apart] by four horses).
17. "Shorn table" is the literal French meaning of *table rase* or *tabula rasa*.
18. In French *pair* (even number) and *père* (father) are homophones.
19. *Aigues*, from the Latin *aqua* (water), and *Mortes*, French for "dead". Aigues-Mortes is a French town on the Mediterranean coast not far from Nîmes.
20. "Devastation — the pretty schoolgirl".

# CARDINAL POINT

*For Georges Limbour*

# I. BLOOD AND WATER ON EVERY FLOOR[1]

*... in order to restrict the traffic of those bodies.*

I was at the theatre. A little girl dressed in white had just gone up to the foot-lights and asked:

"Where is Augustus?"

The actors, speechless, looked at each other in astonishment; the villain, his plans thwarted, staggered off the set; and the hero and heroine, making up once more, hugged each other to the applause of the auditorium, the entire audience rising to its feet in order to acclaim a *dénouement* which reconciled so ingeniously the sacred principles of Religion, the Family, Country, Capital and Work.

I was waiting for the curtain to fall on this grand finale, shielding the actors from the prying enthusiasm of the crowd, when I was surprised to discover that however simple my prognosis, it was not going to be realised.

The curtain remained poised, forever poised, while the set gradually darkened, as if a sheet of nothingness had been dropped in front of it, casting the entire scene on the other side of the bright footlights into blackness, like a balcony over an abyss.

The auditorium steadily emptied, however — as if nothing had happened — and I could hear people congratulating each other as they went out on what a pleasant evening it had been. The usherettes in their scarlet caps covered the seats with grey dust-cloths without paying any attention to me, my eyes still transfixed by the illuminated footlights which now separated the double night of the stage and the auditorium, a beam so powerful that in it one might risk the tremendous, death-defying plunge or the perilous acrobatics of the high wire — when reason is no more than a thread, a thin wire stretched between two poles which one thinks one has mastered, while below there is the emptiness of the unknown, where unseen spectators huddle together to admire your dance-like exercises, the phenomenal curve of your thighs and your craftily padded breasts always tipped with aphrodisiac points of red chilli.

I remained standing therefore, suitably attired in my evening suit, a top hat under my arm, waiting until the auditorium was completely empty before giving myself up to the idiosyncrasies typical of my singular temperament. The last usherette had gone home, but there was still some noise in the corridors and I could hear the sound of the cashier stashing away, as he did every evening, part of his takings somewhere in the basement of the theatre.

That man had once been my friend. His name was Alfred and he kept a number of dancers as mistresses. He always wore a black skull-cap, which he kept on even while making love, had a wrinkled stomach like a suitcase full of mean sentiments, which would hardly have sufficed to fill a purse, and a droopy rod completely lacking insight, incapable of imitating a plumb-line, when the sex verifies the architecture of a love founded on the quicksands that hour by hour destroy the verticality of its walls.

I had fallen out with this imbecile over some love affair or other: a woman I had supposedly stolen from him, while for more than a year he had been salting away a quarter of the daily takings in order to replace with money the jagged medal which some people have in place of a head and which everywhere serves them as an official pass. I knew him to be capable of the blackest treacheries, and I did not want him to surprise me accidentally in the course of the mysterious journey I was about to undertake behind the stage of the great theatre, by way of the drab staircases which lead to secret boxes where beautiful women titivate their legs with the impeccable rouge of their blood and the armature of their shoulders, raised like drawbridges immediately prior to an assault.

When every sound had died away, and the chink of gold under my feet remained only in my head, I decided to leap across the orchestra pit, clearing the luminous barrier in one bound — and landed on my heels on the stage, now separated from the auditorium by a portcullis of light which isolated me as completely as a waterfall in the dark grotto into which I had ventured.

From the fly-floor above the stage there hung some foliage which I could not see but whose shape, still smelling of printer's ink, brushed my face. I was unable to understand how the set could have changed since the end of the play, the last act occurring in a drawing-room, and I switched on a small torch to see where I was.

The furtive light cast by the bulb revealed some woods, or rather some imitation woods, in an English park. Smooth trunks rose up unsteadily in the cold wind which threatened to uproot them, and on the side furthermost away I discovered some fragments of posters and obscene inscriptions.

How had this landscape substituted itself for the furniture which had cluttered the stage only a short time before? I could not say. The best explanation I could come up with was that a careless stage-hand, accidentally pushing a button on some control panel, had caused this canvas and paper vegetation to spring up in a moment, with its dusty yet greasy odour, an odour the dampness of the atmosphere only amplified, and which complemented the smell of sweaty skin and cheap make-up which the three hundred actors and actresses had left behind them like the sea whose retreat leaves cast up on the shoreline old, rotting seaweed, broken ends of bottles and pieces of bone.

I crossed the stage cautiously, apprehensive of falling through some trapdoor which might suddenly open beneath my feet and swallow me up perhaps for ever in the subterranean labyrinth of the theatre, amidst rusty claps of thunder and lightning machines, entangled in the rigging lines and incapable of escaping from those invisible bonds lest my slightest movement unleash a series of artificial cataclysms the least serious of which would lead to my immediate discovery.

As I continued, I thought of the *Ingénue* of the play. I recalled certain tones of her voice and the desire slowly awoke in me of penetrating her dressing-room in order to steal some small article of toiletry — a powder-puff or an eye pencil — that I could cherish as though it were as precious as a drop of her blood, the indelible redness of which only fades in us as it gives way to the hues of death.

The *Ingénue* was a pretty coquette who would innocently turn up her skirt in order to grant a glimpse of the frilly petticoats underneath — white like a clock face around midnight, as piercing as the winter wind, as delicate as the hands which smooth them so gently as to be frightening or reduce one to tears.

Perhaps it was for her that earlier I had leaped over the footlights that separated me from vertigo, for her that I had waited for the usherettes and the members of the audience to slink back to their lairs, even if I imagined that I had only been attracted by the lure of the abyss, when I thought I had seen the set metamorphose into the desert which precedes the whole of creation.

I could not hope to reach this girl's refuge at my first attempt, but counted on the help of a miracle or else of some secret instinct which would take charge of my sense of direction.

Already I had the feeling that this retreat would only be found in the upper reaches of the theatre, in the very highest part, the least accessible and the most remote, separated from the stage by a labyrinth of corridors and staircases, dimly lit by occasional gas lamps whose pallid glow would put to flight mice, rats and other more secretive animals.

I turned automatically into a narrow corridor, the walls and arched roof of which were decorated with naked women — the same naked woman repeated a thousand times over in the same posture: the right leg depicted on one wall, the left leg on the other, and her sex on the keystone from which hung an oil lamp whose flame occupied the place of the pubic fleece. These torsos stretched out above my head, as pink as old leotards whose mendings were represented by cracks in the evenness of the colour, and the same face every ten paces smiled at my hair, which I could feel undulating as if it were being caressed by a real breath.

As I went forward, this hallucination became more precise: I was no longer walking along a corridor of stone, but between the thighs of a living woman with innumerable doubles, between the parted thighs of the tripping, ingenuous coquette whom I was tirelessly pursuing through the labyrinth of her ruses. I admired the palpable suppleness of her body, and even wished that her shiny feet would move further and further apart — until they were so far apart that the keystone of the vault would come down to the level of the floor and crush me to death in a vice of living flesh, wood and rubble.

Meanwhile, my hair was undulating more noticeably, I could see the walls breathing and the lips part under the influx of blood, revealing white teeth like the battlements of a fortified town at the centre of which floated a red flag of tongue. Her breasts became swollen until they almost touched my forehead, her hair brushed my face, and smooth arms snaked around my neck, proffering flamingo-pink nails.

I no longer knew where I was, and I wondered whether I was not still in the artificial forest, the theatre making me the plaything of its mysterious fauna or the captive mirages of the desert. The tattered posters and graffiti I had read on the backs of the trees had changed into tattoos on the skin of the naked woman. The entire history of the world was drawn on her body, the floods and earthquakes reduced to the proportions of organic accidents and ethnic migrations represented by simple changes of name around a heart pierced by an arrow. The voyage of the Argonauts ended a few inches from her sex; the Hundred Years' War with its knights in armour hid under the nails of her left hand; finally, in her right hand, there resided the people of the greatest nations:

| | |
|---|---|
| the Atlantes | for the thumb |
| the Cimmerians | — the index finger |
| the Mayas | — the second finger |
| the Egyptians | — the third finger |
| the Pelasgians | — the little finger. |

I had just finished deciphering the history of the War of the Slaves, when I felt several drops of a thick, burning liquid fall on my lips. At the same moment I saw a bead of shimmering milk standing out on the point of a breast close to my mouth. I collected it on the tip of one of my fingers in order to moisten my lips, but as soon as I had done this, the entire body disappeared, there were no longer any legs, nor sexes, nor hair — and I found myself once again at the end of the corridor, at the bottom of a small staircase, while on the screen of my memory there appeared, with the sound of a gentle flutter of wings, a faint lapping sound, the word:

FRIVOLITY.

With a pounding heart, I ran up the stairs, leaping from step to step without worrying about the creaking which suggested the likelihood that the staircase would collapse, and soon I came across a tiny door which I was sure was the entrance to the den of the *Ingénue*, the girl with the beautiful body and shimmering reflections who had enslaved me with her foolish caprices, by the arches of her eyebrows, as ecstatic as the rising sap…

"Chess-board less dear than white bread, world of height in direct relation to its fragility," I exclaimed, "one must think of hunger *as this snow*. That is the gem of determined action which saved the evening, the gardener by birthright who burns scalps, when our delicate linen, health and joy are massacred. By fire, by sea, by fire, remember this name:

*Blind-mystery-without-equal-my-birth-and-time*."

With one blow of my fist, I burst through the door which blocked my way.

But I hesitated a moment on the threshold, keenly surveying what was offered to my eyes, a new corsair avid of proof.

On a bed on the far side of the room, wearing only her stockings, a woman was sleeping, like an animal ensconced in its shell, and her sex slept too, like an animal ensconced in its shell. The walls of the room were whitewashed, the thighs of the woman were as pale as white lead; and, in the very middle of the room, an enormous plaster finger which was pointing towards her gaping sex jutted out through a crack in the flaking ceiling, drawing towards it the swirling molecules and lines of perspective. Horizontally, a tiny ball the size of an egg was moving through the air, rebounding silently from one wall to the other, sometimes passing close by the naked woman without waking her.

In the sleeping body I recognised the *Ingénue*, and I was burning to go and stroke her, but I remained completely immobile, waiting until she opened her eyes before I approached her.

However, I heard the door grate as it closed behind me, making me a prisoner of the room which an ominous flame caused to dance before my eyes. The finger remained pointing in its immutable direction, the sphere continued its mysterious journey at the same regular pace, and I panted, standing in my costume of another world from which the black sheets of the walls provided me only the slightest protection.

Then I noticed the *Ingénue* who, her eyelids still closed, with an obscene movement of her hand indicated to me the porch of her thighs. I understood that her gesture was intended to draw to my attention the only way out of the room. With clenched teeth, I flung myself upon her — but as soon as I had reached the centre of the shell, I forgot about time, space and the theatre, because a tongue snapped me up like a mill-wheel and swept me away in the muddy water which flowed between two industrialised banks lined with gas-works and coal heaps.

# II. FROM THE HEART TO THE ABSOLUTE

*... a thin cluster of light black lines.*

A slight shock, the birth of a fissure which extended with the sound of torn silk, and I found myself again lying beside a river full of wood shavings and strips of tanned skin drifting down towards the brine of the Arctic seas.

In the caves of the Earth, thieves were heaping their treasures and counterfeiters were heating iron rods in order to mint coins bearing effigies of the dead. I no longer remembered the *Ingénue*, nor her deceits, I only remembered a bound, a rapid ascension and that dizzy fall through the recesses of a womb whose infinitely multiplied meanderings had led me to this place.

The landscape around me was desolate: without vegetation, just stones, stones and a few clouds. I noticed far away some abandoned quarries and stationary wagons. Every sign of wealth seemed to have crawled into the bowels of the Earth, from which issued forth the sound of raised voices, quarrels and the blows of picks muted by the superimposed stratifications which separated the obstinate seekers from the atmosphere. The air was heavy and motionless, not at all troubled by the caress of my lungs, and I felt it on me — that air which allowed the movement of no bird to be traced upon it — like a glacier with no moraines.

The silence of the surface was hardly disturbed by a gentle, far-off whirr, the only perceptible vibration, to which my thoughts clung as to Ariadne's thread, the last organic ligament which held me suspended above a mineral sleep; and attentively I followed the infinitesimal variations of the sound engendered by that chord, sometimes lower or higher, according to the minute modifications of energy which animated it.

Yet, after a few minutes, it seemed to me that the intensity of the humming sound was increasing, as if the object responsible for it was coming much nearer, nor was it long before I saw a black point emerge above the horizon, a point which soon became a line, and which moved with the direction of the river, hovering a few metres above it and obeying the slightest movement of the water's current. It was a bronze arrow which dragged in its wake a long white streamer on which I could distinctly read:

THE CATALAUNIC FIELDS

At the same time I could see a file of galleys approaching, manned by three ranks of rowers, following the arrow with sails unfurled and their decks laden with armed warriors bearing shields and helmets.

The pikes and the rigging above their heads criss-crossed each other, forming a kind of net which bound the sky, while hanging from the masts, as breastplates might hang from the spinal column, the sails were clearly moulding the invisible torso of the air. I could hear the seamen's shouts and could see the soothsayers circulating among the soldiers and explaining the omens that could be deduced from the game of dice, while dishevelled girls ran from one end of the deck to the other, the prettiest of them twirling flames and knives. All the boats were covered with oriflammes and statues of gods, the largest one bearing a vast canopy of steel links, beneath which rested the Emperor, a thin, trembling old man who seemed bored under his purple mantle and who raised his hand from time to time to adjust his crown while a naked young girl huddled before him. He was protected by several meshed rows of lances through which I could glimpse the glittering of his sceptre, pointed into the air in order to ward off lightning and other menaces.

"*Every exigency derives from human blood,*" the centurions cried, their words punctuated by the toiling groan of the rowers. "*An act of force: iron, fire, the future will be white with marvels.*"

I rose mechanically to watch the fleet pass by, but noticed that my clothes were in rags and spattered with clay and seaweed. I ran away and hid behind a rock, and it was from there that I witnessed the landing of the Roman army, and then the Barbarians' flight, at the same moment as the arrow, which had become separated perpendicularly from the river, planted itself right on top of a little hill — its banderole, which had grown unnaturally long by now, covered the entire plain, hiding in the folds of its nineteen letters the rare undulations of the terrain and the diverse phases of the battle.

I saw THE CATALAUNIC FIELDS stretching before me like a body of water swollen by cataclysms, the furrows rigorously directing the trail of corpses whose ashes were being carried in closed urns to the catacombs. Strange mirage, the U was scooped like an urn — the two Cs, the extreme points of the coulter and share of the plough, cleaving the plain for ell upon ell and unleashing the catapults — and, finally, the S of treason serpentining with the last Barbarian hordes who were vainly mounting a surprise action before falling back in whimpering fear.

When the battle was over, the nineteen letters crumbled together and became encrusted in the ground like memorial inscriptions.

Behind the Roman lines, I could see the Huns in flight, brandishing torches as they ran. Many wagons became stuck in the swamps along the river, whole bands of men were sucked into the earth, and when the tip of the fire-brand they had raised as high as possible had also disappeared, the flame became detached and fluttered about in the form of a will-o'-the-wisp. Thousands of fires burst into flame in this manner in the dying day, while the Roman dead began to blanch in a strange putrefaction that destroyed both bone and muscles, gradually transforming them into glabrous mannequins, sexless, smooth-limbed and with their spherical skulls quite bare, like white leotards stuffed with horse-hair.

The bodies lay about me, before the lances and standards carried by the motionless Roman soldiers, who differed from the dead only in that they were vertical.

When night had fallen, the corpses began to rise slowly in ranks of ten to fifteen and chase the will-o'-the-wisps without any movement of their arms or legs, floating a few metres above the ground. When they caught up with the fugitives, their icy breath extinguished all the flames, and soon all that remained on the plain was rank upon rank of pikes, the Emperor's tent still glittering like a coat of mail in the light of the moon, and the white mannequins stretched out on the memorial letters, blending with them in an identical insensibility of stone, pebbles abandoned in memory, a short distance from the river which continued its course towards the North.

The nineteen white letters gleamed in the darkness, immovable, as if they had emerged from the ground and constituted its suddenly exteriorised skeleton. Mist rose from the river and hovered above the battle-field, becoming more opaque as the night became darker, forming volutes as dense as those of the draining arteries of smoke.

At midnight, the vapours massed immediately above the inscription and wrote in the air:

19

which was the number of white letters, set on the blackboard of night like the first coefficient in a prophetic operation the consequences of which would be felt far beyond the sensorial domain, as far as the extreme point of the needle which sews for us the web of the universe hemmed by our human lives.

The wind buffeted the two numbers and made them dance one in front of the other, like a couple making love. The 9, the more sinuous of the pair, was the woman, offering her round loop to the 1, which leapt up vertically, at times closing in so as to thrust its angle into the circle.

I was watching this comedy for the seventh time when the two numbers permanently fused and disappeared, then there emerged in white against the background of night:

$$1 + 9 = 10$$

The sum having been performed in silence, for an instant equilibrium was restored. But my hearing was suddenly lacerated by a terrible clap of thunder, accompanied by a tremendous bolt of lightning, which divided the number ten and swept the 1 and 9 away, while at the same time shaking the crests on the tops of the helmets and covering the tips of the pikes with numberless sparks. Then the decimated 10 was also annihilated, and in its place I saw the two numbers

ƨ and 5

the first green and the second blood-red, the colour of lips and wounds, represented by a half-naked Spanish woman in a scarlet shawl the design of which emphasised the imaginary lozenge whose vertices were the red hole of her mouth, the pink points of her breasts and the dark stain marking the confluence of her thighs.

Like an object and its image in a mirror, the two fives faced each other, like the eagles on the escutcheon of Charles the Fifth, but the five which was turned backwards dwindled rapidly and there remained only the red Spanish woman who represented the number of the senses, the fingers and of coition.

The dancing woman was angry, a feeling born more of the storm than the rhythmic beat of the number which had engendered it. She suddenly rose, therefore, to her own power, $5^5$ (the number of all the ruses of which she was capable), by drawing from her marvellously fine and smooth black stockings a pair of castanets which she raised as high as her hands could reach to unleash a crackling of numbers which soon crossed the rays of the rising sun.

Facing the soldiers, the dancer with the lozenge made the ground clatter with her heels, her unfurled fan cut the air into five quarters of numbers and landmarks which revealed to me once more that total death, like gestures, is only a combination of angles and a change in direction. At the same time, the teeth of her steel comb marked, by channelling them, the temporal divisions created by the sun's rays. Part of the light was reflected on the pikes of the legionnaires and the dancer amused herself by combining the movements of her fan and her comb in such a way as to increase as far as possible the intensity of the reflected light.

Finally, as she whirled dizzily about, transforming the air into a vast luminous cage which was nothing but interlaced bars, the arms and armour of the warriors suddenly became incandescent, and in a moment the entire Roman army was engulfed in flames. The molten metals sank into the crust of the Earth, suspending the flesh and bones of the soldiers in a state of decomposition, their fossil imprints being found many centuries later in the ingots of that white and unbreakable substance which ignorant scientists call

MARSITE,

mistaking it for those lapidifications of the sky which sometimes burrow themselves into the earth, not having fallen from high enough to cross it from side to side.

Meanwhile, the storm which had destroyed the numbers had now reached its maximum velocity. I stood trembling behind the rising tide of my senses, watching the adventure rapidly unfolding.

The galleys fled, resembling a flight of cranes. The sun became the slowly spinning chamber of a revolver which at regular intervals revealed a body lying like an arrow in the mouth of the barrel. A shot rang out every minute and the body, its hair streaming ahead, would be lost in space. The dancer disappeared at the moment I was about to grab hold of her, and the whole landscape was swallowed up and replaced by a gleaming maelstrom with spirals more dense than the wood of a crucifix.

I was hurled into this whirlwind from whose heart there issued from time to time a multi-coloured bubble which would knock against the zenith, smash itself to pieces with a great commotion and return to the funnel in the form of splinters of mirror, pocket-knives and compasses.

Rotating around the polished exterior with me were a dark woman, a goat and a bottle containing some scraps of paper, four crystal dice and a ball of string all pickled in brine. Each time my position with reference to the bottle allowed me to see a new face on one of the dice, the woman stretched out her bare arms and the goat shook its beard, while a bubble emerged from the funnel.

It was the woman who was the first to fall into the central vortex; I was still some distance away when I saw her totter and disappear with a long cry, like a torch going out. The goat followed her almost at once, but was fortunate enough to encounter one of the bubbles, which carried it rapidly into the air; there it changed into a cloud, which enabled it to descend without injury in the form of a fine rain.

As for myself, at the very moment my circular motion was about to bring me to the brink of the abyss, I managed to grab hold of the bottle and, by shaking it violently, I was able to throw a 12 with the dice, which placed me under the protection of the Zodiac. Within reach of my hand, as it happened, I found an aerial girdle decorated with the twelve signs. Of its own accord it wrapped itself around my loins and bore me away from the maelstrom, transporting me far from the Earth's gravitational forces.

When I returned to this planet, it was on a beautiful summer's night; I was transformed into a meteorite, and upon its smoothest surface were engraved these words which summarised everything the number 5 and the oriflamme of The Catalaunic Fields had taught me:

*"Needle*
*a stippled curve*
*here is the thread of thought*
*Celebration at crossing the Equator line*
*— and the Field of the Cloth of Gold*[2] —
*that's where the shoe pinches*
*the circumvolutions*
*in the prismatic shadows."*

# III. THE SIGNAL OF THE ARCTIC

*... the rotting grooves among the boards of the air vents.*

Between the stone walls in which the sexual lozenge of nature held me imprisoned, the principles which constituted my living body were confined. I could hear all the sounds of the Earth thanks to my ears and the crystal nerves in which the fire of the sky and volcanoes circulated.

In order to amuse themselves, three travellers who were going round the world recounted their adventures to each other, and I could hear their words of never-varying pitch as they encircled the Equator with a ring of sound.

"As a spectator at a sports day held on the Balearic Isles in honour of the Doge of Venice," said the first traveller, "I watched the scum of every port in Europe converge on an immense platform, a sinister gang of hooligans in running vests, and heard them shaking with laughter as they slapped their muscles. One of them suddenly jumped backwards, his back towards the void, and fell on his head. He regained his balance still in that position, waving his legs in the air. His comrades fell about with laughter, clapped their hands and pointed at him, saying: 'Look at him boxing with his feet!'

"At that moment, three heralds announced the arrival of an impresario who wished to sign up the boxer-phenomenon. With several blasts on their horns, they caracoled on their horses and led everybody off towards a sort of barn where the remains of a feast were still scattered on the floor. We all sat down, I was in the first row, and when everyone was properly installed the impresario, accompanied by his wife, made his appearance.

"He wore a long, black frock-coat and a top hat. Instead of a head, both he and his wife each had an enormous sphere — upon which the Poles, longitudes and latitudes were all marked — balanced on their shoulders. The continents were outlined in green in the case of the woman and in brown in that of the man; in place of a nose the latter had a compass-dial and in place of a mouth a drawing — set down in the middle of a garden laid out in the French manner with green blobs representing the shrubberies — a drawing which exactly resembled the plans of a fortress in the time of Vauban; the fortifications were painted in pink, the centre of the fort white, and on it was inscribed in antiquated letters:

***PORTE ROYALE***

"The two terrestrial globes were so transparent, as if made of a very fine gauze, that I was able to see that the man and the woman were black, or rather black terrestrial globes, because the globes were an integral part of themselves.

"The impresario began to make a speech. After some general remarks about the laws governing the sensations and feelings of a man being dependent on the position he occupies in relation to the direction of rotation of the Earth, he congratulated the boxer-phenomenon for knowing how to hold his head down so well; then, suddenly addressing me, he asked why I wore my hair cropped short. As I remained mute, he explained what he meant, while his wife, in order to help me comprehend the meaning of his words, took hold of my right hand and, forcing my fingers into various positions, pressed them against the dome of her head as if to mime the successive stages.

"I was quite right to wear my hair cropped short, the impresario told me, since in that way I had a head of hair which was mineral, and not vegetable as are the majority of heads of hair. Progress towards perfection occurs by way of mineralisation; consequently all great thinkers have sought to advance from the vegetable to the mineral by replacing in their minds their sinuous and indecisive roots with the cutting edge of sharp angles. If the German mathematician Einstein prefers the vowel U to the vowel I, it is because the former is mineral while the latter is vegetable. The same applies to the inscription on the cross of Jesus Christ — INRI will become UNRU[3] when the Kingdom of Heaven is established across the face of the Earth.

"The impresario went on to describe in detail the metamorphosis of every object present. He explained how his watch-chain, which started out as a chain of creeper tendrils, had transformed into a silver chain; then how the rope of the service-lift in the corner of the room had mineralised with age and desiccation.

"The principal causes of human mineralisation were, according to him, the make-up women apply to their faces in order to give themselves the lustre of marble, and the consumption of alcohol and drugs. Alcohol transforms the extremely malleable wood of thoughts into a wood of iron, then into the stone of the *idée fixe*, the final, most solid pedestal on which we can perch ourselves. Drugs lead us to the great purity on the other side of the abyss, to the apparent insensitivity of porphyry that runs through rare congealed veins.

"This peroration was the occasion of my first disaster. As I seemed to be having difficulty in following its progress, the negress suddenly placed my index finger on the Pole of her head. I felt a tremendous shock, and with a scream I fainted.

"When I came round, I was no longer in the barn, but on board a slave-trader scudding towards the Indian Ocean. I was asleep down in the hold, my wrists and ankles fettered with irons which completed my mineralisation by their contact and the complete immobility which they imposed on me. Whiffs of vegetable odours none the less reached me, and I could already imagine the naked Indians, with their sexes of tropical creepers in which snakes concealed themselves."

"In an industrial city which sucked in the flames and vapour of the sky through the long mouths of its chimneys," said the second traveller, "I entered, one evening, a brothel of white chalk in order to escape the horror of the streets in which there walked only men with dry, calcified tongues.

"The largest room was square-shaped, built entirely of a pale stone and almost transparent. From the ceiling, hanging by a metal wire, a brilliant sphere was suspended which swung with a slow, perfectly regular motion a short distance above the floor. Under the zone of oscillation of this pendulum, a circular basin had been worn in the very stone; on the slab at the bottom could be seen the dial of a compass on which the directions N-S and E-W were marked by two deep channels which crossed in the middle, each wide enough and long enough for a man to lie down in comfortably. On the side of the basin were engraved these words:

ON A GILDED BED

THE BRELAN

**AUTUMN**

by its savour

AND ALWAYS

*the red zone*

"A little old woman, whom I immediately took to be the madam, explained to me the use of the metallic pendulum and the compass-dial.

"According to the custom of the house, each pair of lovers were to unite four times in the trough of the basin:

"once, lying in the E-W channel, head pointing W, that is to say parallel to the Equator, face turned towards the Occident, in the opposite direction to that of the rotation of the Earth;

"another time, lying in the E-W channel, but head pointing E, that is to say parallel to the Equator, face turned towards the Orient, in the same direction as that of the rotation of the Earth;

"once, lying in the N-S channel, head pointing S, that is to say perpendicular to the Equator, face turned towards the South Pole;

"a last time, lying in the N-S channel, but head pointing N, that is to say perpendicular to the Equator, face turned towards the North Pole;

"and during this time the pendulum should not cease to mark time above them like a metronome.

"The madam also informed me that the girls read portents according to the way in which their lovers made love to them and the order in which they effected the four cardinal operations. It was for this reason that they had given a name to each of these positions: the first, facing the setting sun, was called *Slope of Memory* — the second, facing the rising sun, *Future Prospects* — the last two, *Ill Fortune.*

"I made love four times with a pretty enough girl, a fine carpet in which I embroidered my blood, then I left for the North again, preferring the torment of the ice and polar mirages to that of artificial fires and sullied fantasies."

"As for me," declared the third traveller, "I know the Pole, the real Arctic Pole whose roundness is as taut as a forehead, its heart of stones or fibres of granite, wakes of wings of spume which make the wheel of the senses turn. Concerning this journey past or future, I have written on paper an account as close-packed as the universe. Listen! and let each of my words bury themselves in your hearing to mould the ingots submerged there, the subterranean veins of memory marked with fissures and occurrences, the arteries of cerebral marble as cold as the ice-floe carried towards the stars, lights of liners full of men, ropes and merchandise.

*... The man had disappeared, the eddies caused by his fall had dissipated and I could no longer see a single hair of his beard floating in the current; but a placard had now been uncovered and I could make out certain letters — as black as crevasses under a thick layer of snow — constituting a marvellous advertisement:*

*FOR SALE*

THE PRESENT

*STATUES REJUVENATED*
*THE NUMBER*
*HAIR CARE*

IN THE MOUNTAINS

perfect milk

**VISIBLE FIRE**
**AND THE NORTH**

the genuine way to make yourself look beautiful

*Just as I finished reading it, a hand came out of the river: it belonged to a sleeper who had come to the surface and was peacefully making his way, swimming between the currents without having yet emerged from his sleep.*

*I had no concern for my half-naked companion, whose hair covered me, nor for the pendulum swinging in a glass shop-sign. My only thoughts were for the bearer of this mysterious placard, this sleeper whom I had seen drifting along the river, and my greatest wish was to find his trace, even if it meant my going to sleep for ever. I was in the water in a second, and started swimming with long, regular strokes, pacing myself as best I was able in order to make it to the ice and fire of the North (because I was sure that the trail of the sleeper would lead me to the Pole), the hemisphere veined with blood and solar lightning.*

. . . . . . . . . . . . . . . . . . . . . . . . . . . . . . . . . . . . . . . . . . . . . . . . . . . . . . . . . . . . . . . .

*The water was extremely cold, and I encountered strange currents. Sometimes I felt myself being sucked under from below, and it was all I could do to resist. Later, seaweed entangled my limbs and I had no idea how to free myself. The river was full of greenery: the fauna and flora of the entire world must have gathered for a reunion there, and when I had escaped from the treacherous caresses of the dormant plants, I bumped against fish which stabbed me with their razor-sharp fins. It must have been a very long time since I had set off, hours or even days perhaps. I felt close to exhaustion and could hardly tell if I was still breathing. As I went on, the fauna became more abundant, and more dangerous too: I frequently glimpsed a milky octopus lurking at the back of its lair; as I passed near by, it lazily extended one of its tentacles, and it was only by a miracle that I escaped being ensnared; sharks chased and fought each other under my very eyes, shellfish opened their luminous valves and crustaceans ripped my flesh with their armour.*

*Later, the water became still colder. It seemed to require a much greater effort to master, an increasingly viscous element in front of me had to be displaced: I was no longer swimming in a river, but in the Earth, between layers of strata. What I had mistaken for spume was nothing less than a froth of rock crystals, and the seaweed weighing me down was the fossilised imprints of ferns in a seam of coal. In order to clear a path, I had to push aside an incalculable mass of minerals; I slipped in the auriferous sands and my legs became covered in clay. My body must have had imprinted on it, to the furthest branches of its veins, the imprint of every known form of stone and vegetable. I had forgotten everything: the sleeper whose trail I had wanted to follow, the pendulum, the house, and even why I had set out on this adventure.*

*The shelves of matter pressed down on me ever more tightly, threatening to transform my mouth into an air vent. I was hardly advancing and years must have passed after each of my strokes. I had skirted unknown springs, drunk from geysers of stone. My body appeared to me as no more than a tiny lucid point in the Earth's equation. The world grew rich with filigree, a succession of opacities and transparences so subtle that my eyes could hardly distinguish them. I believed I was travelling along a line, that I myself was nothing more than an abstraction, a number attached to the outside of a curve, spinning dizzily about its own axis. Fast and slow no longer held any sense for me and I was unable to tell whether I was stationary, or the needle of a compass swinging at the speed of light in the direction of the Pole.*

*Meanwhile, I could feel the path I was following shrinking beneath me, becoming ever more difficult, and such was the cold that I thought I must be a prisoner in a capsule of ice which had begun slowly to suffocate me.*

*In the end, I was no longer even concerned about keeping going, only about freeing myself, for the mirages had dispersed and I now knew that I really was caught in the ice, crushed by an ice-floe, as confined as the pendulum under its glass casing. I suddenly recalled those birds which dilate every cavity in their bodies in order to approach the sun. Gathering all my forces, I inflated my veins and viscera; my bones flexed like bows between the poles of death — and the block in which I was imprisoned exploded with a terrible sound, projecting me with absolute self-knowledge as far as the foot of the Arctic Pole.*

. . . . . . . . . . . . . . . . . . . . . . . . . . . . . . . . . . . . . . . . . . . . . . . . . . . . . . . .

*The Arctic rose before me like a cupola, a mountainous balloon or the dome of a head. Luminous cracks of varying sizes split the ice to its furthest depths, converging towards the summit, so that it looked to me like the veins which furrow a skull.*

*Noticing the Pole shining on the ridge of this mountain, I climbed its hemispherical slope, convex skull-cap of the Earth, letting myself be guided by one of the brilliant crevasses, my fingers clutching at the hardened snow. I was almost at the summit when I heard a far-off voice close against my ear turn into crystal with these words:*

*I knew immediately that the voice could only be the sleeper's and that she was speaking to me of the polar cracks, the original fissures of angles and bearings. I understood the mystery of migrating birds, of atomic energy which defies the forces of gravity, even the egg which breaks asunder in the heaven and on the Earth. The oracle of the pendulum was revealed to me in all its obviousness — and I learned at last the true goal of my journey, for this tide of light was so bright that it caused me to scream — shrill, bitterly cold, the very cry of the Arctic — while my body toppled through space ever further away from the Pole,* V<br>E<br>R<br>T<br>I<br>C<br>A<br>L<br>L<br>Y.

With a pale, frozen face, the traveller stopped speaking after this word, the letters of which fell upon me like the molecules of a dagger dropped point first when it plants itself quiveringly in the ground.

I immediately felt my stone cells distend, and getting to my feet on regaining human form I stood to attention when I heard this appeal:

VERTICALLY.

The voice of a mulatto woman then rose up from the depths of a Californian brothel, a voice full of stones, birds of prey, animal pelts and gold mines; and I heard the single cry of a couple without hope, two lovers who had departed for the Antipodes one after the other and who had met halfway in order to kill themselves, at the moment of their reunion, with a single shot of a revolver.

# IV. THE SEVENTH ARRIVAL OF THE NIGHT

*... then the flight of something obscure and unwilling.*

In my mind, just like the ghost of an edifice reduced to the fishbone of its walls, the voice was propagated obliquely, a long arrow fired diagonally. Under the momentum of the magnetised head aimed at I knew not what problematical point, my ghost began to swell, continually extending its boundaries. How far would it reach? How far?

Buffeted by the vegetal waves of this sinuous voice, imaginary walls began gradually to appear and their skein could be seen like the venous network of circulating blood. Imperceptibly, the ghost increased in volume, devouring all the emptiness, and the walls dissolved in this nothingness, ceaselessly being forced apart and stretched more thinly by the lengthening of the arrow, whose tip alone changed place, growing ever darker and moving ever higher.

The report of a pistol reverberated from space to space, and I could hear the projectile's whistle as if, in an upward spiral, it had gravitated around the arrow, like a satellite. But the arrow, soon out of all proportion, faded away, melting into the entire universe, and the only sensation which remained with me was that of the vanished walls which persisted in trying to materialise, solicited by the monstrous voice.

Buoyant as the incoming tide, the voice rose up with maritime and volcanic catastrophes, cyclones and lava-flows of perceptions, which impregnated the air with long sulphurous deposits that soon dissolved into clouds and meteorites. The scarlet ball of love slithered along the voice's imponderable axis, every fantasy being displayed in the deep cracks of this armour whose joints allowed the thoughts to show through. It was a bloody, vital voice, and first of all there was a scurry of messages from my left which fled towards the desireless horizon, with the great clamouring of birds of the night:

"*Paris* → 18,25 — 51. 623 — 8. 281. 718. 312,001 → *Vancouver*.

Cashier Alfred absconds with Théâtre-Français Ingénue. Tracks found. Palm Beach Police. 6 million missing."

"*Lutetia* → + VI — CXLIX : DXXI + 4, ΣΘ → *Persepolis*.

General Aetius inflicts heavy losses on Attila. Barbarians routed. Populus Romanus for ever! Cheerio!"

"*Savannah* → 2 — 18-0,37 392 — 2,7 — X (black numeral) → *Pasadena*.

Professor Jackson of Fisk University for Blacks has invented process for transforming rotten teeth into gold teeth on the spot, without extraction. In the same manner Miss Bricktop[4] changes animal voices into porphyry voices."

"*Spitzbergen* → $0^{\circ}\ 60'^{\,\mathrm{VI}} < 4/5 < 125\ {}^{\mathrm{oo}}/_{\mathrm{oo}}$ → *Tierra del Fuego*.

North Pole lost with all hands. Morale at low ebb. Clash of icebergs against prostitution of outbreaks of fire. Many thousands of cathedrals submerged, bell clappers replaced by fish. Alphabet sacrificed on glass altar."

"*Equator* → 1 . 2 . 3 . 4 . 5 . 6 . 7 . 8 . 9 . 0 . → *Equator*.

Lost: protean lozenge. Description: piece of string, woman's hip, watch-spring, meteoric disc, sun-spot, oil well, beauty-spot, mathematical formula, oral coitus, meridian of taste, end of smutty word, nervure of utterance, maze of screams, diced fruit, flocculous number. Rolling-mill of images is superfluous."

Then the messages began to talk among themselves, and I could hear the echo of their discussion:

"Reason is the plate and the heart of the fork. What is the dish?"

"At the point of a lance, a crystal parapet. It is quite clear that this parapet cannot but be the memory or the desire."

"The sensorial odds and ends on our chimney-breast, a furious wind blows birds trailing in its wake. Of what are these birds?"

"They are made of white soot and clouds of rock-salt."

"Word and respiration linked, language stifles you. What do you shout?"

"I run through my ivory or pewter vultures with lances, on an azure field of sand or unsheathed sabre."

"What did you do at the snows of yesteryear?"

"I flew into the air, others soiled themselves."

"To have a love of action, why does one not say: to have an action of love?"

"O passion! Pushed on by you, I pass for active, I act passively."

"Higher than the white cadastral survey of the lunation, how do the dead mark the boundaries of their domain?"

"They mark their angular sojourns with ash and shards of blood."

"And you, what do you inscribe on your domain?"

"Magic zebra of fire, here the knife becomes trigonal. It escapes and is forever scoring the dawn, mosquitoes and the rumpled scarves of the gilded marsh. Sudden squall soaked in salt and sea-water, sweat-matted hair, O voracious sister… Curvaceous agility, I inscribe: VOCABLE with my mouth."

"Whited number, who has darkened the sky?"

"The writing of my movements. Solidified words in the air which discolour the washerwomen's linen; their consonants are the elbows and knees of these women, who beat the rivers' breast with mortifying caresses, and whose movements rip the air with invisible injuries which will later bring into being the flash and the parabola of meteorites."

"The sweaty sheets of death hang from the worm-eaten framework of Euclidean geometry; a single movement would quickly turn them into centipedes. Do you know which are the fairies these unclean and venomous animals torment?"

"The stars mask the ghastliness of time's gaze, and throats rise up in trajectories of burning metal, between the vanquished pillars of material anxiety. There will be wild beasts and statues, judgements making love like boomerangs. Broken ideas, aerial constructions will set themselves up on the scaffolding of our vertebrae, far beyond the polar cold of these waves despoiled by monsters, the rational imbecilities with which you pursue me, a cripple susceptible to the frost."

As soon as they had heard these words, all the messages pounced on the one that had uttered them and there followed a free-for-all of shouting and pecking, from which the letters, flying out with the feathers, began to flash as they escaped from this crucible stoked with anger. The fiery characters, halfway through a parabola, remained fixed in the air, and once all the messages had torn each other to ribbons, two enormous luminous notices became visible in the sky, the first at the zenith, the other halfway up:

For the
REDUCTION
OF FORMALITIES

*MURDER AND FIRE*

THE CREATOR
OF TRUTHS

is tracked down in the woods

BY PHOSPHORUS

victorious nature
WELL ENDOWED

DROWNS ITSELF

*PAST* *PRESENT*

gentle skin
rosy cheeks

A STARK NAKED BODY

IN ORDER TO MAKE
YOUR HENS LAY EGGS

*Available everywhere*

Then the voice began to swell, gradually becoming menacing. The illuminated sign of the stage bar which harboured its source was violently shaken by a sudden gust of wind and began to swing, projecting across all the public buildings the inscription *Silver Dollar* in white letters against a red background, and the glint of a silver dollar. A black cloud of smoke rose in the air, then fell to the earth as a saffron powder which delivered unto man the commands of the clouds.

"When satin banderoles flutter on top of the Towers-of-Silence-in-the-Desert, electric aigrettes crackle in the vaginas of murderesses, and bluish thunderbolts lodge in the battlements behind which kings shelter, with their crowns of geometric shapes and white lines etched upon the black background of their seals. In the meantime, squatting at the back of the casemates, the guards rattle dice in their helmets and question the twenty-two cards of the tarot:

the *Fool* is a man with neither highs nor lows, with neither right nor left,
the *Juggler* a tattooed negro beating the drum,
the *Popess* a naked woman,
the *Empress* a whore who masturbates with a sceptre,
the *Emperor* a murderer of little children,
the *Pope* an old man wearing a dunce's cap,
the *Lover* a boxer,
the *Chariot* a locomotive, Stephenson-type,
*Justice* a procuress with red hair,
the *Hermit* an idiot,
the *Wheel of Fortune* a table of logarithms,
*Strength* a submarine,
the *Hanged Man* a skeleton,
*Death* a rolling-mill,
*Temperance* a Folly,
the *Devil* a total black prick,
the *House of God* a mouth,

the *Star* a nipple,
the *Moon* a woman without a head,
the *Sun* a head of hair,
the *Judgement* a catastrophe,
the *Universe* a sex hardened between the fingers of chance."

"Pronoun without attributive," replied a cloud as white as the quicklime which eats into dead bodies. "I intone an imperative verb through infinite syntax. The correspondence of tense and the formation of improper fractions of adjectives of quantity are gutturals. Euphemism contextualised by the interrogation of a past anterior, the liquid consonants are silent, in spite of the vague interjections which describe the ellipses, metaphors and parables. Passive liaison of genres, formulated in the future or gerundive mood, the perfect and the imperfect conjugate in a great proposition of place expressed in diphthongs. 1, 2, 3, 4, 5, 6... numbers are the defining parentheses of glimmers of light, a pleonasm of words of which every series is ordered as a consequence of pleonasms, discourses with identical fragments, without attention to construction, by syllabic elision of the number (mode) of analysis or synthesis."

"More simple than the division of areas and the fall of bodies, the multiplication of loaves and fishes may be explained by considering the + signs formed by the scales of the latter and the – signs formed by the cracks in the former. Plus times minus makes minus, as everyone knows; thus, the multiplication of the loaves by the fishes gives rise to a negative aliment, that is to say nutritive by its material absence, which is indicative of divine sustenance. The same applies for the mystery of the tree of the knowledge of good and evil, in which the entire tragedy is acted out between a man, an apple in the shape of a zero and a snake biting its own tail in order to become a horizontal eight representing infinity."

"Under the blue gaze of time, the kaleidoscope, the eternal return and the curve of the universe converge their distant or major lines at the cabaret of souls. Signs show through the clay sides of the pitcher of space which contains a liquid that seeks only to disperse, signs deformed by the undulations of the surface and the rules of refraction. Bread and water, which are the vertical and the horizontal, engender fish, then disintegrate them into layers of oil which carry into houses cold fins of light and the scales of conflagration. And on the body of this fish born of the flesh and blood of directions, a cross may be seen, image of the masculine principle, the positive number, and plague-infested houses..."

Thus spake the clouds in their language of thunder, without managing to drown out the voice whose vibrations oscillated between two poles (of love and of the mind) and strained to substitute the hard crystal edges with damp seaweed and carnivorous flowers of love, replacing the frozen, dead plains of the rigid mind with tropical adventure in a warm grass-belt.

In my mouth, mine of words and kisses, thoughts and desires became confused, reduced to the unique expression of the utterance, and I knew no more than to modulate the syllables in the same way as did this voice, the sensitive caress of ideas immediately torn to shreds.

The silver coin suspended below the sign, liberated from its chains by a gust of wind, rose into the air like a new moon, then disappeared, gnawed by the corrosive acids the stars secrete. The skyscraper, churches, brothels and theatres were engulfed, demolished by the carnivorous voice which devoured earth, wood, iron and the magnetic waves of water and fire. The universe was soon no more than an enormous, spear-shaped leaf, each vein of which should have corresponded to one of my adventures, and on the point of which the voice was perched, like the figurehead of a woman who helps the bows of ships cut through water or the drop of poison with which certain negro tribes envenom the tips of their assegais.

The bullet from the revolver had stopped gravitating and, still stained with the blood of those it had killed, sped along each vein, emphasising the passage of the sap like a red indicator.

In the first vein I saw myself as I was when I was pursuing the *Ingénue* through the labyrinth of her gestures which beat for me time's tempo. My body was a great clock regulated by a menstrual flux which stained the world with colours alternately crude or pallid, according to the degree to which the tide was affected by the attraction of the moon; my head was no more than a hollow bell periodically ringing to precipitate strokes coming from outside. I had arms like rods on which the curtains of action glided. I wanted to become completely mineral, to be nothing more than a simple stone capable of making fire at the first strike of a finger-nail.

After the second vein I no longer knew what I was.

A blade of straw, the mobile corner of a lip, the wake of a boat *en route* for the Levant, a musical note played on a grotesque instrument, a fragment of food misplaced during an official banquet, a church wafer, the flower in the buttonhole of a hooligan, the pink knee of a prostitute, an animal in a prehistoric forest, a Yankee soldier in the American Civil War, a Roman haruspex, the astrologer who predicted the first Great Plague of London, a piece of bone gnawed by the neighbourhood dogs, a powder-compact, a blunderbuss, a sextant, a final full stop placed at the end of a mathematical treatise, an imperfect subjunctive, a comma, a row of dashes, the couple supposed by that row of dashes, an old binding with a cracked spine, a postage stamp in the collection of a millionaire, a shield left by a Crusader before the Holy Sepulchre, a scarf forgotten in an enclosed field, the collision of a train and a herd of cattle, the strips that wear and tear detach from a globe of the world, a length of ribbon given as a love-token, the last breath of a mirror, the lustre of a marvellous skin and the imagined look of a blind man, all of those things I was at the same time, plunged into a confusion which only a voice could help me escape.

However much the finger indicated to me the curve of the veins, they were for me still no more than the abstract signs under which any object could be hidden. The leaf was a whole desert, or an agglomeration of monsters which seemed all alike to me, in the abolition of all human hierarchies. But the voice, that utterance madly in love with itself which I called *Body and Soul*, had pulled me into its sphere. It had detached itself from the top of the leaf which had now withered and lured me on after it, into the emptiness of absolute space. I remembered the bodies stretched out like an arrow which I had seen being launched by the rotation of the sun and the vertical fall of the polar traveller, whose verbal expression had liberated me from my gehenna of stone. All the kings and all the loved ones formed a circle, a crown within my head, a ring I would never be able to hang on to, even on my heaviest finger. But these memories were soon dispelled, and I then found myself completely alone with the voice.

My tongue became as inert as a red flannel rag, the direction of my gaze fell like a slack rubber-band, all my senses grew numb at the same time as my brain, and it was only after having submitted to this tragic end and having forever parted company with the mind's unreliable artifices that I had the final perception of my limbs dispersing — a real Jericho reduced to dust through the love of a voice — while my true being liberated itself, assuming to the eyes of the shadow the appearance of a fragile scaffolding of letters, itself ready to collapse at the faintest hint of breeze:

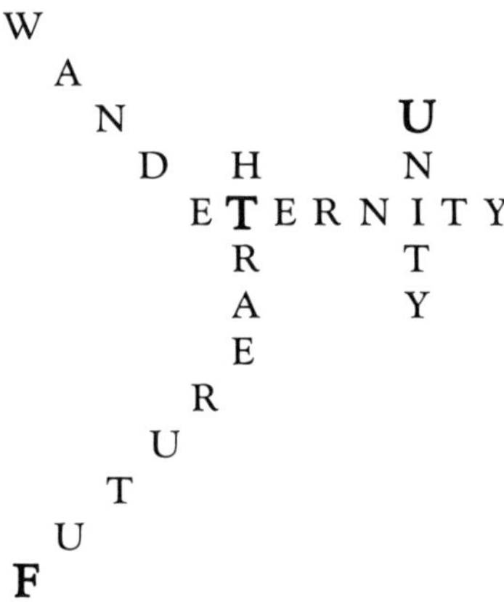


Paris,

October 1925.

## NOTES

1. The title of this opening section is clearly inspired by the plaque which all new buildings in Paris carried from the 1890s onwards: *Eau & gaz à tous les étages* (Water & gas on every floor). Plaques, signs and advertising hoardings frequently made a strong impression on the Surrealists. André Breton and Philippe Soupault's *Les Champs magnétiques* (1920), for example, closes on the notice which was frequently to be seen outside bars in Paris: *Bois & charbon*. Robert Desnos's *La Liberté ou l'amour!* (1927, and also published in Atlas Press Anti-Classics) is presided over by Bébé Cadum, a monstrous smiling baby used to promote a brand of soap at the time. As late as 1958, Marcel Duchamp would turn *Eau & gaz à tous les étages* into a readymade.
2. Near Calais, the scene of an unfruitful meeting in 1520 between François I and Henry VIII. The name refers to the magnificent display of the two monarchs.
3. INRI, the initials of the Latin words said to have been placed on Christ's cross, often appear in Christian art: *Jesus Nazarenus Rex Judæorum* (Jesus of Nazareth, King of the Jews). UNRU is derived, presumably, from the German word *Unruhe*, meaning "disorder", whether of a private mental kind or public unrest.
4. Ada Smith (1894-1984), black American jazz singer who settled in Paris in 1924. She managed a club on the rue Pigalle for a while before opening her own venue, The Bricktop, on the other side of the street in 1926. Leiris knew both establishments well. In a little-known article written in German the same year, he remarked that Ada Smith often got involved in long conversations with a "black intellectual" by the name of Jackson who accompanied her on the piano. Leiris was perhaps more than a little fascinated by Miss Bricktop, and her name appears several times in his *Journal*.

ATLAS ANTI-CLASSICS

1. THE AUTOMATIC MUSE Novels by Robert Desnos, Michel Leiris, Georges Limbour & Benjamin Péret. *Out of print*
2. 4 DADA SUICIDES Texts by Arthur Cravan, Jacques Rigaut, Julien Torma, Jacques Vaché
3. BLAGO BUNG BLAGO BUNG BOSSO FATAKA! German Dada from Hugo Ball, Richard Huelsenbeck & Walter Serner
4. OULIPO LABORATORY Texts by Claude Berge, Italo Calvino, Paul Fournel, Jacques Jouet, François Le Lionnais, Harry Mathews & Raymond Queneau. *Out of print*
5. MALPERTUIS The modern Gothic novel by Jean Ray
6. THE AUTOMATIC MESSAGE Texts by André Breton & Philippe Soupault, and Breton & Paul Eluard
7. THE WAY HOME Longer prose by Harry Mathews
8. ADVENTURES IN 'PATAPHYSICS *Collected Works of Alfred Jarry*, Volume I. *Out of print*
9. THREE EARLY NOVELS *Collected Works of Alfred Jarry*, Volume II
11. WINTER JOURNEYS by the OULIPO (see 18 below for new augmented edition)
13. NEW IMPRESSIONS OF AFRICA Raymond Roussel, illustrated by H.-A. Zo
14. THE DOLL Hans Bellmer
15. CIRCULAR WALKS AROUND ROWLEY HALL Andrew Lanyon
16. LIBERTY OR LOVE! and MOURNING FOR MOURNING Robert Desnos
17. AURORA and CARDINAL POINT Michel Leiris
18. WINTER JOURNEYS by Georges Perec and The Oulipo (Michèle Audin, Marcel Bénabou, Jacques Bens, Paul Braffort, François Caradec, Frédéric Forte, Paul Fournel, Mikhaïl Gorliouk, Michelle Grangaud, Reine Haugure, Jacques Jouet, Étienne Lécroart, Hervé Le Tellier, Daniel Levin Becker, Harry Mathews, Ian Monk, Jacques Roubaud & Hugo Vernier)
19. THE TUTU Léon Genonceaux
20. DON'T TELL SYBIL George Melly